Whitewater Run

Thinking that being on the run can be no worse than the torment of phoney incrimination and punishment, Billy Finch escapes from the brutal prison of Great China Wash.

Riding many miles south, a vengeful search leads Billy to Walnut Bench and its sheriff, Bigg Harmer, who, in a serpentine twist of fate, is seeking the same man. Billy decides to strike a deal and joins a posse of hard-bitten gunmen and outlaws with prices on their heads in a thrilling, action-packed trip across the border into Mexico.

Whitewater Run

Caleb Rand

A Black Horse Western

ROBERT HALE

© Caleb Rand 2017
First published in Great Britain 2017

ISBN 978-0-7198-2572-9

The Crowood Press
The Stable Block
Crowood Lane
Ramsbury
Marlborough
Wiltshire SN8 2HR

www.bhwesterns.com

Robert Hale is an imprint
of The Crowood Press

The right of Caleb Rand to be identified as
author of this work has been asserted by him
in accordance with the Copyright, Designs and
Patents Act 1988

Typeset by
Derek Doyle & Associates, Shaw Heath
Printed and bound in Great Britain by
CPI Group (UK) Ltd, Croydon, CR0 4YY

CHAPTER 1

The hot, dry spell had ended, and lightning fizzled silver, cracking the darkness that enveloped the Mohawk Peaks.

Astride his grullo mare, Billy Finch shivered, stared blearily ahead as he rode from the foothills. When his head fell forward the rain still drove in. It dribbled from the strands of his long, corn-coloured hair to his neck, then around to his mouth and chin. It was difficult to recall a time when it wasn't raining, like he didn't know for sure how long he'd been in the saddle.

It was near an hour later when a cluster of low-lying buildings became visible ahead of him. He rode on, into the town with the sound of rain slanting against the clapboards, the ghostly glow of windows in blacked-out stores.

A wedge of yellow light shone from the false front

of a saloon, and he knee'd his mare forward to the hitch rail. He stood quiet for a few moments, listened to the hiss of rain on the spreading puddles, pondered on getting himself down from the saddle. He peered further down the street, looked to a short rope that swayed above the entrance to Antigos Livery. With doubtful thoughts he squeezed his eyes shut and moved his horse on towards shelter.

Small oil lamps barely lit the features of the man who was seated inside the livery. He made a slow, heavy-eyed assessment as Billy dismounted, then turned back to the range saddle across his knees.

'Leave your horse. I'll tend it when I'm through,' he said, his stumpy fingers moving deftly at the stitching.

Billy made a thin smile. 'I hope there's some people in this town a little more considerate of business.'

The man's pale rheumy eyes looked up, this time a little more conciliatory.

'Thank you,' Billy continued. 'What do you charge for all the trouble?'

The liveryman took in the hard humour of Billy's words, the broken nose, dark stubble under the shapeless Stetson. 'Dollar usually covers it.'

'That sounds fair. Suit you if I pay when I come back? I'll be wanting to see you haven't loved it to death,' Billy mused. 'Besides, I can't say how long I'm staying . . . if I'm staying.'

The livery man's tongue darted along his lips. 'I'm guessin' it'll have to be OK. But you sound like you've got an honest face.'

Billy nodded an acknowledgment and shouldered his saddle-bags. At the entrance he stopped. 'Is this town called anything? It's not mentioned on a map.'

'Walnut Bench.'

'I was figuring I might be in Mexico,' Billy said. He looked at the meagre lights from the buildings opposite the livery. Half-way up the street he could see the distinctive bars that fronted the green glow of a roller-blinded window. At the next flash from the sky, he saw the sign hanging outside the sheriff's office.

'You're a full day's ride from the Gila river. I guess that'll be behind you, to the north,' the liveryman said. 'Nogales an' Sonora are about the same, ridin' south. That help?' There was no reply, and when Sam Antigo raised his eyes from working the leather, Billy was gone.

When he was almost opposite the law office, Billy stood quietly in the shadows. A figure stood profiled in the light that was spilling on to the street.

Deputy Franklin Poole stared dully at the rain as he lit a cheroot. 'Not much of a time to be out and about,' he said, over his shoulder, apparently to no one in particular. 'Even the coyotes stay clear o' this goddamn place.'

A couple of minutes later, after several puffs on

his cheap smoke, the deputy went inside. The door was pushed to, extinguishing a shimmer from the dark standing water.

Billy walked on past a hardware store, glanced fleetingly at his own reflection in the shadowy glass. Alongside a lighted doorway he tensed slightly. It was an open beanery, its sole customer sitting on a high chair hunched over a coffee mug. The man's broad back was straining around a short, cloth chaqueta. Under the pulled-down hat brim, there wasn't much to see. But dark hair, thick neck and assured posture made Billy curse under his breath.

Blinking shocked surprise, the man stared wildly, turning around to make a grab as his Stetson lifted. 'Hey, what's the hell's goin' on?' he yelled.

'Sorry,' Billy said, grinning awkwardly as he replaced the hat on the man's head. 'I thought I knew you. Real sorry.'

'I'll give you sorry. I was just about to drop off there . . . kind of a precious moment.' Now standing, the man was a head taller than Billy and half as wide again.

'If you were me you'd have made the same mistake. No harm done. Don't make a fight of it,' Billy said quietly.

A slight change of stance and a flinty hardening in Billy's eyes, settled the swarthy man's attitude. 'Wouldn't be much o' one,' he mumbled.

The dark-featured waitress behind the counter

chuckled tolerantly. 'Come on, drink up, Tipper. I want to close,' she said.

'I'm goin'. Coffee's like bear piss, anyway,' the man remarked lamely. On his way out he gave a sneering laugh. 'One minute, mister, that's about how long you'd have lasted if I'd been in fightin' mood.'

'He's an Irisher, an' a bag o' lard,' the girl told Billy, 'though I wouldn't like to take a serious right-hander from him!' She picked up the coffee mug, emptied its dregs and balanced it on a small pile of unwashed crockery. '*Mañana*,' she decided and smiled wearily across the dirty counter.

'Odd times my pa was left to clean up, he'd say, "It'll wear clean",' Billy offered. 'Maybe you know the feller I'm looking for?'

The girl leant an elbow on the counter and supported her weary face. 'Looks like our Tipper Rourke from the rear does he, this feller?'

'Yeah, he does. A few years younger, maybe. Similar disposition.'

The girl loosed off another short laugh. 'I'm sure.'

'He can be talkative ... sometimes,' Billy said seriously. 'And he dresses fancy. Partial to a certain grade of woman and gambling.'

'So what the hell would he be doing here? Friend o' yours is he?'

'I know him well. Have you seen him, or anyone like him?'

The girl shook her head. 'No. I think I'd remember. Sounds like you'd do better asking at the Cabaña. That's where you'll more likely find those interests of his.'

'The Cabaña? Yeah, I think I noticed it. Thank you,' Billy said. The lingering odour of fried meat and chile stirred the need to eat. But weariness from a dozen hours in the saddle, and the chill beneath his sodden duster, required some other nourishment.

'Meeting him's important is it?' the girl asked.

'To me it is,' Billy replied flatly as he walked back into the rain.

Rose Jaula yawned, her eyes straying back to the pile of dirty dishes. She looked at the clock, shrugged and removed her apron.

As she reached to douse a lamp, she heard the light clinking sound of conchos behind her.

'You forgot somethin',' the tall man standing there told her.

'No,' Rose scowled. 'It's gone eleven.'

'By nearly ten minutes.' Franklin Poole smirked, draped his lean frame on the stool vacated by Tipper Rourke. 'Us peace officers don't go by clocks. Where's that feller from . . . the one who's just left here?'

Filling a mug with tepid coffee, Rose didn't hide her dislike for the deputy. 'No idea. He didn't say,' she replied.

Poole shook his head. 'Bigg's pullin' out tomorrow for a few weeks. I'll be the big wheel 'till he returns.'

'Big wheel? You?' Rose scoffed. 'You'd make a better music hall clown!'

'Huh, what do you know?' the deputy muttered, staring down at the coffee mug. 'You wouldn't say that if I was sheriff proper an' permanent.'

'I'd be making some fitting noises, though.' Rose laughed into the man's face. 'But seriously Frank, you'd make it real tempting to be a bad man.'

'Very funny – it's you should be on the goddamn stage.' Poole sipped the cold coffee, swore and spat.

'If I wasn't so scared of catchin' somethin' nasty, I'd smack your face, you pig,' Rose sneered.

Blood pulsed in the veins around Poole's temples as he slammed the underside of a balled fist against the countertop. Moments later he moved to leave, then paused, clenching and unclenching his bony hands.

'Did he have a name?' he demanded.

'He's going to the Cabaña,' Rose replied. 'Why don't you follow and ask him yourself? Tell *him* you're soon goin' to be Walnut Bench's big wheel.'

Once again Billy crossed the street of water and mud. He stepped on to the skimpy walkboards and shuddered involuntarily. In the last fifteen minutes the town had grown darker, colder, more miser-

11

able. Of the few lights that pierced the darkness, the brightest was that breaking over and under the swing doors of the Cabaña. He heard the discordant sounds of a honky-tonk piano and a drunk, cursed and turned to look behind him as though hoping there was something better. Instead he saw something momentarily move beneath the overhang of a narrow-fronted store. He stood very still, listening and peering into the darkness. There were a few louder notes from the piano and he turned back to the saloon. The doors were being pushed aside and Tipper Rourke's bulk thumped out.

'Well, look who's here,' the big man slurred, seeing Billy almost immediately. 'My night ain't finished after all.'

'You're not still looking for a fight are you? For chris'sake get lost,' Billy rasped angrily. His thoughts were occupied by whoever had been moving in the darkness further along the street.

Rourke focused on Billy and zigzagged towards him. 'Ain't got no cactus flower savin' you now, boyo,' he continued clumsily.

Sidestepping Rourke's befuddled charge wasn't difficult. Nevertheless the man's fingers clutched and held on to Billy's sleeve. Struggling to shake the grip, Billy saw a tall figure step down from the boardwalk opposite.

Almost at a run through the rain, Deputy Poole waved his arm. 'Stay where you are,' he yelled.

12

Billy cursed, looked towards the mouth of the alley that sided the saloon. He moved quickly, twisting towards the deeper darkness.

'Gimme a fight, goddamn you,' Rourke cursed.

Billy gritted his teeth and drove his knuckles hard at the hand, then the wrist and arm that was dragging him back. Then he punched the fleshy face that was at the same level.

He ran from Rourke into the alleyway, straight into a stacked pile of empty crates. Alongside at head height, a single window threw feeble light into the darkness. Billy hugged the saloon side, stepping quickly past for a few more feet and stopped to listen.

Beyond the weatherboards, the piano banged away, and an accompaniment of raised, raucous laughter. Billy crouched, shivering against the rain tumbling almost invisible from above. A shadow flitted across the coloured side windows, and he heard boots squelching mud.

'Come out o' there . . . whoever you are,' a voice demanded, and Billy cursed.

'I just want a few words,' the man continued. 'If there's nothin' you ain't doin' or done, there's nothin' to fear.'

Yeah? Go to hell, Billy thought. The Prescott judge had been clear about the penalty intended for Billy Finch, and lawmen were mostly lawmen, wherever they were. And a short length of rope dangling above a livery wasn't too far off a necktie.

Billy stepped back, edging slowly away with one hand trailing flat against the weatherboards. But the pursuer followed, and for a moment Billy saw his shadowy form as he passed the side window.

The solid slab of a doorstep met the heel of Billy's foot. He swung his hand back, searching for a doorknob. He found one, but it wouldn't turn, and cold sweat immediately stung his eyes.

The squelching footsteps approached again, and he hit the door with his shoulder. But it held, and he turned, moving his hand towards his Colt. He took a few short breaths, and stared into the darkness as the lawman got closer. Then he heard the sharp, unmistakeable click of gun hammers being actioned.

He dropped to a crouch and moved away, and continued to where he thought there would be a dead end. But instead, the alleyway bent into an even narrower turning.

At the same time, someone pushed up a sash window from near to where he'd just come from. 'Who's out there? This ain't common land. Clear off,' an irate voice squawked.

In the sudden shaft of weak light, Billy caught a glimpse of the surprised lawman. 'None o' your business,' Franklin Poole shouted back. 'Get your head back in.'

Billy wasn't for pressing his luck. He went with the alley, continuing quickly, looking for the first left turn and back to the main street.

The street was deserted, and contained little more than the lights from the saloon. While he watched, the beanery went dark and Rose Jaula appeared on the boardwalk. Billy waited until the night concealed her, then he quickly crossed the street.

There was another alleyway almost opposite. The short, dark passageways all did the same thing: containing trash and disused store materials, they ran to the rear of the buildings that lined the street, then turned parallel. Billy got his bearings, twisting right, then right again. He emerged at a point further up the street, directly alongside the Walnut Bench saloon.

Rubbing his upper arms for circulation, Billy peered from the dark opening alongside the saloon to the yellow aura that spilled outside its batwing doors. With the rain easing off, and satisfied the deputy was still searching behind the building, Billy strolled casually along the boardwalk. With the strains of the honky-tonk piano playing to a silent street, he looked into the bar room, but couldn't see Tipper Rourke. The long counter was littered with empty glasses that the sour-faced barkeep was pushing into a cluster. The roly-poly piano player stopped in the middle of a tune as Billy entered.

The barkeep hardly bothered to look up. 'Yeah, that'll do, Curly. Best part o' the day's ended,' he added as though for Billy's benefit.

'This town's sure light on civility,' Billy said. 'It's something you notice when you're tired and come a long way.'

The barkeep looked up, eyed Billy's damp, bedraggled clothes. Because he couldn't see if there was anything covered by the slicker, he nodded. 'You're right there feller. Nevertheless, I hope you ain't a slow drinker. Whiskey?'

'Yeah.' Billy shook his head tolerantly and leant on the bar. 'Two or three fingers.'

'Someone askin' for this stuff at midnight nips my curiosity,' the barkeep said, betraying the faintest of smiles.

Billy tipped the shotglass empty and grinned. 'Nothing unusual there,' he agreed.

'So who you lookin' for?' the barkeeep continued.

'How do you know I'm looking for someone?'

'The haunts of most God-fearin' folk are closed down. Besides, I've seen the look before.'

'I bet.' Billy waited until the shotglass brimmed again. 'His name's Tyler Quince, or *was*. He's got good reason to be called something else.'

'He was Quince when I met him.'

Billy's knuckles whitened around his glass. 'Met him? He was here?'

'Easy feller,' the bartender laughed thoughtfully. 'I'm talkin' of more'n a year ago.'

'Do you know where he went? A year ago?'

The barkeep shook his head. 'No. But wherever

16

it was, he took our sheriff's daughter with him. If he'd to show himself back here for more'n a minute, he'd be dead meat.'

Disappointment showed instantly in Billy's face. 'You've no idea where he went?'

The barkeep didn't answer, and Billy followed the man's gaze to the figure who'd just pushed his way through the batwings.

Franklin Poole carried a scattergun and looked serious. 'Strange route to the saloon,' he said, keeping Billy covered. 'I'm guessin' you've got some sort o' hogleg under that slicker, so put it on the bar nice an' easy,' he commanded.

With a tired shrug, Billy obeyed. He drew out a Navy Colt .44 and placed it carefully on the counter.

'Now clasp your hands in front of you,' the deputy then snapped. 'You carryin' any other weapon?'

Billy thought for a moment. 'There was a girl in Plumtree thought so. She said I was a menace to her and her frail sisters.'

Almost smiling, Poole brandished the barrel of his scattergun, an indication for Billy to move towards the saloon entrance. 'It's a short walk. Don't try runnin' off again,' he said flatly.

There were shimmering veins of far-off lightning, and a low rumbling murmur, like a run of startled cattle. The storm had passed over and beyond Walnut Bench, and now broken cloud revealed a big silvery moon.

'Goin' to be a good day for some. Start walkin',' the tall deputy snapped.

Billy walked ahead, along the hushed street to where a half-open doorway glowed with lamplight.

CHAPTER 2

Sheriff Bigg Harmer hated being alone with his floor-standing pendulum clock. He thought it was in cahoots with the working of his heart – a signal of his life ticking away. His joints pained him every time it rained, and old scars from old fights tightened across his leathery hide. Pain often showed in his grey eyes, but not all of it was physical. He looked around the office where more than thirty years had somehow disappeared, the unadorned white-washed walls, the short rack of hand guns, the sagging canvas cot, two scoured, empty cells.

He squealed the swivel chair into a full circle, slid open a drawer in the heavy, mahogany-topped desk. Sifting beneath a pile of wanted dodgers, he drew a photograph of his daughter into the lamplight. For a moment, the hard, weathered lines of his face softened – but then he heard a boot scrape, the jingle of a spur from outside, and he quickly pushed the drawer closed.

'Bigg. Lookee what the storm's blown in,' Franklin Poole said, pushing his captive through the doorway.

'What law's been broken this time?' Bigg Harmer asked, yawning.

Poole tugged Billy's Colt from his belt and banged it on the desk. 'This ain't a stick o' candy,' he said by way of an answer.

'No, it's certainly not,' Harmer acknowledged, but looking up at Billy. 'What else?'

'Maybe circumstantial, Bigg. He's a tad badge shy,' Poole explained. 'Minute he sees me, he takes off into the nearest alley like a scalded cat.'

'Since when was that against the law?' Harmer commented wryly. 'Sit down, boy. The good deputy's eagerness sometimes gets the better of him.'

When Billy was seated, the old sheriff continued. 'Now, what's the trouble? What *were* you runnin' from?'

Billy took an easier breath. The anxiety and anger at being made to walk at gunpoint to the law office was almost unbearable. Now, the tension eased a little in the presence of the calm sheriff.

'I tangled with a big Irish drunk outside the saloon,' he said. 'Next thing the deputy here's running straight at me waving what could have been a six-gun. Some of the places I've been through recently, I wasn't waiting to find out if he was the

Paddy Roughhouse sidekick.'

'He's talkin' of Tipper Rourke, an' it's not the way I saw it,' Poole protested.

'Shut up, Frank,' the sheriff said, trying not to show the sign of a smile as he looked at Billy. 'Not that you'd know it, son, being short in town an' all, but Rourke ain't got sidekicks. Didn't you see Frank's shiny badge?'

'No sheriff. Maybe if he'd been carrying a lamp, I would've.'

Poole made a noise in his throat as he released the hammers of the scattergun.

'Yeah, maybe,' Harmer said, now taking a closer, more appreciative look at Billy's Colt. 'So, what's the problem, Frank?'

Poole's reply started with a guttural hawk. 'I was doin' my job,' he said. 'It's easy to make it sound futile after the event.'

The deputy's scratchy temperament, the fact he still held a scattergun, didn't help Billy's ebbing anxiety.

The sheriff turned his chair through a half circle. 'You have a name, son?' he asked, having taken a conspicuous look at the empty cells.

Billy considered for the shortest moment. 'Bill Newton.'

As though expecting the untruth, Harmer nodded. 'Yep, an' I'm Abe Lincoln. He lifted the Colt, pointed it at Billy's chest. 'You're Billy Finch. That's the truth of it,' he added, decisive and sharp.

21

Billy stiffened in the chair, his fingers tightly gripping the tips of the armrests. 'What truth?' he answered back. 'Where'd you get Billy Finch from?'

'I'll show you. He's in here somewhere.' Harmer rummaged in the desk drawer while the ticking clock emphasized the tense confrontation. A moment later he pushed a dodger at Billy. 'Yeah, here he is . . . Billy Finch,' he said. 'He's wanted for killing a rancher up near Big China Wash, a couple o' years ago. Look familiar does he, *Mister Newton*?'

Eagerly, Franklin Poole circled the desk. 'Hell, if this ain't the piss an' wind man, Bigg. On your feet, you murderin' sumbitch,' he rasped, knocking Billy's hat off.

'Cut that out,' Harmer barked, now swinging the Colt towards Poole. 'I'll decide if there's to be any rough stuff. Right now there isn't.'

His jaw grinding, Billy stared down at the likeness of himself. At once, it took him back to a nightmare moment two years previous. He felt the rise of his bile, the resentment of knowing Tyler Quince was riding somewhere ahead of him.

'A fat reward for bein' dead or alive,' Harmer said, picking up the sheet and waving it at Billy. 'Shame you ain't him, eh Newton? I guess there'll be nothin' for you just bein' a lookalike.'

Poole grunted in astonishment as Harmer tore the reward notice in half, then into quarters. 'What the hell, Bigg? You crazy?' he blustered. 'What're you doin'?'

22

'I need him.' Harmer threw a disdainful look at his deputy. 'This town's real short on men with sand. I learned that a year back when I tried making up a posse . . . proved it every day since.' He looked directly at Billy. 'What do you think, Newton? Does a thousand dollars sound a reasonable incentive for hunting down a murderer?'

Billy nodded. 'Yes, Sheriff. On the surface, it certainly does.'

'Well, no one else hereabouts thought so,' Harmer said with distaste. 'I had to look in other places.' He put Billy's Colt down, pushed it across the desk. 'You get the gist o' what I'm proposing?'

Taking back his gun, Billy kept his voice calm. 'What's his name, this man we'll be going after?' he asked, already knowing the answer.

'Tyler Quince,' Harmer replied quickly, his breathing suddenly heavy, his voice thicker. 'You know him . . . heard of him, maybe?'

'No, never,' Billy lied. 'How many men did you get from those other places?'

'Four. You're the fifth.'

'Hmm. I'll accept your proposal. And if you'll allow me, Sheriff, I'll have a little something on account,' he said, striding towards the deputy.

Harmer gave a rough chuckle. 'Just remember this is still a law office, Newton.'

'Pick up my hat,' Billy told Poole. 'If you want, I'll make you use your teeth,' he threatened.

Fear filled the deputy's eyes. He cursed, swinging

the stock of the scattergun up into a wild, dangerous arc.

The thought that an inch or two nearer would have given him a badly broken face, made it easier for Billy to drive a fist hard into Poole's gut. A short, hammered right then thudded the deputy against the wall. The man half turned, his nose spraying bright flecks of blood against the paint.

'Now you're even. Leave him be an' I'll show you where you're bedded,' Harmer said to Billy. 'I'll keep the image o' that picture in here.' The sheriff tapped his deeply wrinkled temple. 'Don't forget it,' he added.

'I won't. Nor the thousand dollars you mentioned,' Billy said. With a wry smile he picked up his hat and banged off the dust.

'Come with me,' the sheriff said, taking a ring of keys key from a small pocket on his waistcoat.

Billy glanced at Poole who was scowling, unsteady on his feet, blinking some focus back into his eyes.

'You think the deputy's fit for duty?' he chaffed.

'He's recovered from worse,' Harmer snorted, unlocking a rear door. 'The others are just like you, Newton – they need money, an' to use Frank's words, they're badge shy. You'll have a lot in common. Bring your traps an' stay close to me.'

From somewhere not too far away a horse nickered at their approach. In the darkness, Billy could see a broken down adobe wall that was spiked with twisted strands of barb wire.

'Used to be a holding for prisoners travelling to the Yuma Pen,' Harmer explained. 'Tonight it's your personal boarding house.'

A squat, stone shelter nestled beneath the dilapidated wall. In its deeper shadow stood a slight, unmoving figure.

'Ike Delgado,' Harmer said quietly. 'He's too mean to sleep. Either that or too Wanted.'

Delgado was short and very thin. He wore a narrow-brimmed Derby, and his tight boots moved him slightly off-balance as he walked towards them. The man's general resemblance to a night heron made Billy cuss with surprise.

'Got another recruit, Ike,' the sheriff greeted him. 'Give him fixings an' a bunk, will you?'

'Yeah. How many more we waitin' on?' rasped the slightly built outlaw, his beady eyes glistening as they looked in Billy's direction.

'Newton here's the last,' Harmer replied. 'Him turning up's about timing and chance. Make sure you're all ready. We clear town before daylight.'

'Ain't too soon for me,' Delgado muttered. 'Holed up with these wooshers is worse than doin' hard time.' He gave Billy a second appraisal and sniggered. 'You'll find out what I mean,' he added.

'I'll settle the livery bill an' get your mount brought over,' Harmer said as he walked away.

Delgado took a step closer to Billy. 'Kind o' strange, belonging to a badge toter, Mr Newton.'

'Is it? You tell me,' Billy said sharply. 'I don't

belong to anyone. There's a thousand reasons for me standing here.'

'Obviously we're all gettin' the same.' Delgado scratched a vesta against a doorframe to light the remains of a stogie. 'Come on inside.'

A muscle under Billy's cheekbone worked hard. He thought Ike Delgado made remarks, and asked and answered questions too fast. Like a man who didn't want to rest anywhere for too long.

'This is where we eat.' In a curious gesture, Delgado flicked cigar ash on to an unscrubbed pine table, then he pointed at another doorway. 'There's a spare bunk in there,' he said. 'I'll leave you to it.'

In the light of a single, happy jack lamp, Billy made a meal of gluey, warm beans and a wedge of bread. He drank cautiously from a crock of Pass whiskey, and contemplated his immediate prospects while Delgado prowled restlessly outside.

Moving into the other room he could just about see an unoccupied bunk. He was dry and warm enough, but he didn't remove his boots to lie down. The sweat of outlaw had a tang of its own and hung heavy around him. The darkness was thick and strangely comforting, and he closed his eyes for a moment.

Billy always thought that when their trails crossed, he would have the advantage over Tyler Quince. The score would be settled on his terms, not be within the gift of a town sheriff. Now, listening to the discordant snoring around him, it occurred to Billy that Bigg Harmer was astride a powder keg. He was in little doubt the lawman intended to kill Quince, and it stopped him from dozing off.

The key twisted and relocked the door. From the sheriff's swivel chair, Franklin Poole scowled as Harmer entered.

A water basin and bloodied towel lying across the desktop induced a cold smile from Harmer. 'You bullied the wrong feller this time, Frank. What does it take for you to learn?'

'It ain't a fun matter. I'm still a law officer, god-damnit.' The deputy's voice was hoarse with anger.

'You deserve what you got,' Harmer grunted back. 'You push too far an' someone'll push back . . . wearing a star or not.'

'This ain't finished, not by a long shot, it ain't,' Poole exclaimed vehemently. 'He broke my nose.' The man's eyes cabled resentment across the room. 'Our deal still stands, don't it Bigg?'

'I said it, didn't I? Word o' the sheriff not good enough for you?'

'Yeah. I guess I need it repeated.' Poole tried a crooked smile and winced, ran his fingers cautiously round his nose and cursed.

'An' get out o' my chair. Keep your ass out of it until I ride out.'

'OK,' Poole squawked at the partial confirmation that Harmer was leaving town. 'You still leavin' in

27

the mornin'?'

'Yeah, after what's left o' the night.' Brushing past Poole, Harmer took his seat. 'Get rid o' this stuff,' he rasped, indicating the bowl and stained towel. 'If you haven't finished bleeding, do it somewhere else, goddamnit.'

Poole cast an eye towards the rear door. 'I'll be out back if you need me.'

'Yeah, like a catfish needs sun. If you see Newton, stay well clear. Remember he's now packin' a rod.'

Stamping to the rear door, Poole turned the key, thought for a moment and looked back. He saw Harmer had his back to him. It was a plain sign of contempt, and his intended dissent withered instantly. But his hand had dropped to the butt of his Colt. Sweat broke across his temple and he trembled. His Colt remained in its holster, and Bigg Harmer didn't look around when the door banged shut.

The deputy threw the water basin and its contents across the back alley, a string of curses cutting the air when he saw his hands shaking in the moonlight.

'Evenin' Mister Deputy,' Ike Delgado called from the shadow of the stone shelter. 'I've been expectin' you.' He waited until Poole walked over to him, then led the way into the low building. He produced a bottle from a recessed shelf, and filled two grimy mugs. 'Horse piss,' he sniggered. 'But it's better than nothin' this time o' day or night.'

Poole brushed the proffered mug aside, lifted the toe of one spurred boot to the bench. 'Keep it. Good liquor's available anytime I got a thirst,' he bragged.

Delgado shrugged and drank greedily. He wiped a dribble away from his chin, stared openly at Poole's puffed-up nose. Congealed blood rimmed the man's nostrils and the flesh had started to darken.

'Somebody give you a kickin'?' he mocked.

Poole grunted, looked towards the doorway beyond Delgado's narrow shoulders. 'Newton asleep?' he responded, keeping his voice low.

'He's there. I don't know about sleepin'.'

'Well, it won't be for long, either way.' Poole grimaced. He knuckled the table, peered beyond the flickering lamplight. 'I've decided to meet your price,' he said.

Delgado nodded. 'I figured you would.' He went to refill his mug, changed his mind and took a pull from the bottle. 'Let's see now. One off Harmer, and two from you. That's just about three thousand.'

'Yep, all in good scrip,' Poole emphasized. 'Money like that'll buy you much liberty, Ike. You just come back from Mexico *without* Bigg Harmer, an' it's all here waitin'.'

'I will. How come you don't do your own killin', Frankie?'

Avoiding Delgado's provocative mien, Poole

straightened, stood away from the table.

Delgado did the same and raised a calming hand. 'Hah, don't answer that,' he said. 'How'd you tell someone you've got a white liver?'

Billy crouched very still and quiet in the darkness. He waited until Poole had gone, then he returned to his bunk. He stretched his legs, folded his hands behind his head and peered into the gloom above.

Delgado went back out to his suspicion-filled vigil, and from further across town a rooster started its early crow.

Billy closed his eyes again. *It's even worse than I'd reckoned for Harmer*, he thought. *But that's his problem, not mine.*

An hour later, he blinked from the semblance of sleep. The lean face of Ike Delgado was close, grinning in the low lamplight.

'Pile out,' he said. 'Time for a chew before we ride.'

'Yeah, OK.' Billy gave a showy yawn as he rolled off the bunk. 'Must have been more tired than I thought,' he said, stretching his arms, scratching his head.

One of the men threw a straw pillow at Delgado, then grinned when he saw Billy watching him. 'I'm Clayton Coyle,' he said amiably. 'You the janitor, or are you with us for the sheriff's clambake?'

'Both, I guess. My name's Billy Newton,' Billy replied, but his attention was drawn to the firearm being checked by a stocky, bald-headed man. It was a Yellowboy, sawed off at both ends. It was a specialist weapon, said to combine a pistol's speed with a rifle's power. Billy had seen something similar before, and was of the opinion it achieved neither – although looking the business, he thought it actually ruined a fine piece of gunsmithing.

Flattered by Billy's interest in the gun, its owner introduced himself as Pinky Grill. 'And this here's my fittingly named Mule,' he added, levelling the weapon at the ceiling. 'You want a chimney up there, this'll make it for you,' he boasted.

'You'd think that cannon o' yours was a woman, the way you smooch over it,' one of the others said, and sniggered.

'Well, you'd know, July,' Grill teased. 'Hah. When this feller hits town, smart fellers hide their wives an' lady friends away till he leaves.'

'Yeah. Even the plugs ain't safe,' Clayton Coyle supported.

'What *does* the law want him for?' Grill asked.

'Bein' in possession of a wild bean,' the bald outlaw replied.

'Get up an' out of here, you lazy dog,' Bigg Harmer barked. 'It'll be daylight in a half hour.'

For the next fifteen minutes the men ate in silence, forking cold beans and plugs of fatty bacon into their mouths, drinking scalding coffee tempered with the Pass whiskey.

With an occasional tense look towards Harmer,

Franklin Poole paced backwards and forwards. 'I'm headin' into town, now. You all should be gone,' he said.

'Yeah, deputy's right,' Harmer agreed. 'Let's go.'

After they had filed from the shelter, Poole quickly snuffed out a few happy jack lanterns. But they hadn't all left together.

Holding back so as to be the last to leave, Ike Delgado gripped the deputy by the arm. 'Have them dollars ready when I get back,' he said quietly. 'Otherwise one of us'll be dead meat, an' it won't be me.'

Climbing into their saddles, the group held their eager horses in check while Harmer lifted the gate latch of the old compound. Pale colours of dawn streaked the sky above Walnut Bench as the riders proceeded slowly into the main street. Bigg Harmer was leading, then came Pinky Grill, Clayton Coyle and July Grant. Further back, trailing a pack mule behind Billy, was Ike Delgado.

Franklin Poole hurriedly returned to the sheriff's office. He sat in Harmer's swivel chair, turned backwards and forwards, through the squeal. He jabbed a concho at the side panel of the desk and grinned meanly.

CHAPTER 3

Ezequiel Carlos pointed ahead and shouted: 'Gringos.' His warning brought those trailing behind him in the dusty arroyo to an abrupt halt. They were the Fidel brothers who rode either side of a young, flaxen-haired American woman.

Carlos stood in the stirrups, studying the figures who were cutting along the dry bank of the Whitewater River, almost a half mile away.

'Six,' he announced. 'But we see them, they see us,' he added with a hint of concern. As yet, they were still on the wrong side of the river.

Armando and his brother, Alfredo, looked at their captive. Carlos read their expressions and smiled.

'I shall talk to them, amigos,' he said.

Armando grinned. 'Sweet-talk them, Zeke,' he suggested. 'Gringos fall for that.'

Carlos shrugged. 'Very well. If my lies and your birdsong doesn't get us across the river, our pistols will.' The Mexican saw the young woman shudder violently. 'Calm yourself, *señorita*. It's be quiet or be dead. But there is something worse,' he warned.

Sarah Munnies looked out at the six riders who were now blocking their route to the slow running water. Dust was settling around them, lifting in small puffs and eddies as nervy horses fought their reins.

Remaining silent, the girl lowered her head, pulled loose strands of hair away from her mouth.

Carlos drew a Colt Dragoon and tucked it inside his loose-fitting camisa. Armando and Alfredo also concealed similar weapons as they rode unhurriedly towards the river.

Between the two groups of riders the air hung hot and heavy. The rise and fall of horses' hoofs echoed dully across a charged, flat silence.

Sarah Munnies stifled the panic she felt with the alkaline mud-caked faces staring back at her. She didn't think it was the arrival of rescue or hope, even.

Under the mindful weight of his big Colt, Carlos's heart thumped at the sight of Bigg Harmer. The elderly sheriff was wearing the silver star he feared most in the land.

'*Buen dia señors,*' he started. 'Perhaps not so good for whoever has brought you out from Walnut Bench.' The Mexican dragged up a tentative smile.

'Eyeing the woman, July Grant guffawed 'Fresh

fruit ripens under the sun, greaser,' he said.

'Yeah. Ripe an' ready for eatin',' Clayton Coyle assisted with the ribaldry.

Bigg Harmer's eyes flashed. 'Shut up,' he snorted. 'Watch the other two.'

Ezekiel Carlos's smile vanished at the term 'greaser'. He singled Coyle out with a smouldering glance and the Fidels braced in their saddles. The silence descended again, only broken by the murmur of the river water.

'Where are you going with the woman?' Harmer asked.

Billy noted the lawman's blunt expression, the hasty disgust. July Grant continued his blinkered thinking.

'Us gringos have needs same as them, Sheriff,' he said. 'Where'd *you* think they're goin' with her?'

'I'm asking *him,*' Harmer replied. 'You going to tell me?' he demanded of Carlos. 'Or should I ask the girl?'

'The *señorita is* tired. She lets *me* do the talking for her.' Carlos took a quick, eager look south across the river. 'We're an escort to Pelicano. There is a man like you . . . an Americano, waiting for her. *Comprendo?*'

'Oh yeah, we *comprendo* all right.' Grant guffawed boorishly.

'*Señor,* there is nothing improper here,' Carlos protested. 'She wishes to be with us. She's not a hostage . . . our prisoner. I ask you to let us go by.'

35

Billy had been watching the young woman. 'She doesn't look like she wants to go anywhere with that outfit,' he said. 'She's too frightened to talk back.'

The sheriff nodded. 'Yeah, that's what I'm thinkin'.' He spoke in a strained voice, his eyes boring into Carlos. 'This Americano. He got a name?'

Carlos lifted the corner of his mouth, formed a slight smirk. 'A much important man. A Señor Tyler Quince. Now I must insist we move on.'

Both Armando and Alfredo Fidel gave wide, toothy grins. 'Si. A much important man,' Armando echoed. 'A man we wouldn't want to disappoint,' Alfredo added.

Harmer took a couple of deep breaths while he considered the situation. 'The girl stays. You move on,' he shouted, and drew his old Colt.

Carlos darted a hand inside his shirt, his dark eyes rolling bright and angered. The big revolver came out faster than the sheriff's Colt, but the Mexican's advantage only lasted a second. Two bullets from Grill's gun exploded fatally in his neck and upper chest. Hitting the desert sand hard, Carlos shook once before dying.

Billy cursed at the shooting. The swift, dramatic death of the Mexican made him reconsider his opinion of the hybrid weapon.

Grill himself smiled confidently at his gun's ability. He jerked another round into the breech, fired, and another rider convulsed under the impact of being hit: for a moment, Alfredo Fidel struggled to remain alive, then he wheeled out and down lifeless across the loins of his horse.

Billy heeled his mare alongside Sarah Munnies. He grabbed the reins of her horse, swerved them both away from the deadly lines of fire.

Armando Fidel got off a shot that took a chunk from Clayton Coyle's shoulder. Then he cursed, and gasped as the combined guns of Grant, Harmer and Delgado cut him to pieces. He slumped forward, but remained fixed in the saddle. His buckskin bolted, carrying its burden of a dead rider towards the river and Mexico.

'Stop that goddamn horse – shoot it,' Harmer shouted callously.

Grill was watching. He considered the shot, held the gun firmly in his hands, extended his arms and fired.

Fidel's horse was less than half way across the river when it was hit. The animal snorted and coughed, rearing on ineffective thighs to take another bullet. It fell and rolled with the downstream flood, trailing a muddied crimson wake and dragging the rider south towards the border.

'Get them to the deeper water . . . both of 'em,' Harmer continued. 'We can't have Tyler Quince knowin' what's happened.'

Drenched with sweat and river water, the outlaws dragged both bodies to the middle of the Whitewater before casting them adrift. When they came back for the other two Mexicans, Harmer gave his next instructions.

'Clay, take their mounts. Head back to Walnut an' get your shoulder seen to. If you want to catch us up, OK. If not, we'll handle it without you. Pinky, you get their clothes. They won't be needin' 'em where they're headin'. But *we* might. Sombreros, too.'

When the first body splashed into the water, Ike Delgado saw the sheriff had turned away, was now beyond earshot. 'The ol' star-toter must have five thousand on him somewhere,' he said, as they heaved out the next corpse. 'Why should we wait for our pay off? We got an obligin' cemetery right here.'

July Grant swore softly and smiled wickedly. 'Yeah, the watery grave. Why not?'

Clayton Coyle clutched a bloodied bandana to his left shoulder. 'You goin' to kill the woman too?'

'Hell no,' Grant breathed. 'When was the last time you left the gravy when you were starvin'? Besides, what's it to you? You're goin' to be long gone.'

'Well, I don't like any of it,' Pinky Grill snorted. 'If Harmer ain't packin' the dollars, he ain't worth a bent penny to us dead.'

A moment later they all looked to Billy in thoughtful, silent question.

'Harmer's got no money,' he lied. 'I heard him tellin' Poole he'd stashed it below the border in case any of us got ideas. You can't question the way his mind worked *that* out.'

An angry oath from Ike Delgado ripped the air. 'We can question *you*, Newton. I always reckoned you was his ear man.'

Billy stared down the gaunt-featured gunman. 'No more than you, Delgado. And you've had more time,' he suggested.

'Yeah,' Grill agreed. He raised his hat and ran the heel of his hand across his damp forehead. 'Newton's in the same boat as us. You best get out of the sun, Ike, you ain't thought any o' this through.'

Delgado hawked, trudged irritatedly up the sandy river bank and went to his horse. He pulled a flat quart of Pass whiskey from his saddle-bags and, taking a long swig, let his eyes search out Bigg Harmer.

The sheriff was leading back the pack horse. It had been frightened by the gunfire and had started a run towards the wasteland. For someone wanting to take advantage, Harmer was presenting an excellent slow-moving target.

Delgado gave a quick glance towards the outlaws who were walking up from the river bank. 'Reckon that's the last we've seen of Coyle. There's more chance o' rain than him ever turning up in Walnut Bench,' he called out in Harmer's direction, deciding he would wait for some other opportunity.

The woman couldn't take her eyes off the thinning

curls of dark water, the bodies rolling like sodden logs. The eruption of violence, the lingering, acrid smell of cordite, left her in a daze.

'Take it easy,' Billy said. He didn't like the way she stared fixedly ahead, and offered her his canteen. 'It won't taste good, but right now. . . .'

'Did all that really happen?' she asked distractedly.

Billy nodded. 'Yeah, it happened. These men aren't going to let a small herd of Mexican cutthroats and kidnappers stand in their way. No disrespect ma'am, but right now you're little more than a bonus. Sheriff Harmer excepted. But the worst part's over.'

'Not in my head, it's not.' She took the canteen, drank and offered a thin smile. 'I'm Sarah Munnies.'

Billy nodded uncomfortably. 'Billy Newton. I'm sorry. I couldn't think of anything else to say. Their work means a thousand dollars apiece.'

'Are you all right, Miss?' Bigg Harmer asked.

'Yes. Yes I am. I'd say thank you, Sheriff, but the sentiment doesn't fit,' Sarah said, and shivered unhappily.

'Fair enough,' Harmer bit out, his face remaining impassive. 'Fact is, right now you're a problem we don't need. We're going on into Mexico and there's no one can accompany you back to where you came from.'

'So you're leaving me out here alone?' Sarah

replied with a challenging look at Billy.

Lounging nearby, July Grant chuckled. 'Let's take her with us, Bigg. I'll make sure she don't get lonesome.'

Billy quickly turned on the thickset outlaw. 'Huh. I'd shoot the girl myself, if I thought that was going to happen. Again, no disrespect ma'am,' he added, with a glance in Sarah's direction.

Grant was feeling more secure amongst his friends: 'Sure a lot safer than takin' *me* on,' he taunted.

'That's enough, goddamnit,' Harmer shouted. 'As the young lady's partial to you, Newton, she can be your responsibility. July, you cool down.'

For a full minute, the sheriff of Walnut Bench stared out at the purple haze beyond the Whitewater. 'We'll rest here for an hour. Then we go across,' he decided.

Pinky Grill spread a blanket under the dappled shade of a stunt dogwood. He checked the action of the gun he called Mule, and replaced the spent ammunition.

Grant got to his feet and putted a canon-ball sized rock as far as he could into the river. 'I'll wager none o' you can beat that,' he called out.

'I'll wager none of us is dumb enough to try,' Ike Delgado muttered.

Sweat gathered in the folds of Grant's thick lips as he watched Billy and Sarah Munnies. He saw them walking along the river bank, and immediately experienced a pang of brutish lust.

Billy and Sarah stopped where a stand of sandbar willow hid the river from view. They exchanged a few words, then Sarah pushed her way on through the tumbling foliage nearer the water's edge.

Billy looked around him, and shrugged. He hunkered down, let his head drop for a moment and closed his eyes.

Grant smiled. *Ha, wouldn't be me droppin' off,* he thought. Wanting to be closer to the water, he turned on to his back, dragged himself slowly down the sandy bank. A minute later he stood, crouching below the sandy rise with the river swirling round his knees. Closer to where Billy was keeping guard, he lowered himself into deeper water. He set himself against the flow, keeping close to the shadows cast by the overhang of willow, and moved nearer the bank.

As he stepped up from the water, a pair of flycatchers whistled shrilly, winged their way through the curtain of branches and took to panicky flight. His pulse leapt, pounded when a splash broke the droning silence behind him. He turned, and drew a short, eager breath at the sight of where something or someone had caused a disturbance in the water. Then his foot slipped on a submerged root and he backed off to the tangled curtain of willow. He stepped out of the water and straightened, and gasped when the barrel of Billy Newton's .44 Navy Colt drove into the middle of his forehead.

'You think I didn't know where you'd be, you degenerate son-of-a-bitch,' Billy grated. 'I'd kick you back in the river but you'd poison it.'

Shocked, Grant stared at Billy's gun hand. 'She ain't yours,' he growled. 'For chris'sake, I'd share her. What's your problem?'

'Which hand to use,' Billy replied, and slapped him hard with the back of his left hand.

Grant absorbed the stinging blow. He backed away and a funny little smile crumpled his face. 'Put the gun down Newton, an' we'll scrap for her,' he spat out.

'Yeah, good idea,' Billy agreed gratefully and holstered his Colt.

Billy realized he'd fallen for what Grant wanted, as the man moved sideways. He cursed the moment he was rushed, then again at the weighty pressure pushing him backwards. He stumbled and pain exploded as Grant's knee caught him in the chest.

Billy fell, but twisted and rolled away at the sound of manic laughter. A sodden boot stomped down at him, but he drove out the hard edge of his hand and Grant went over as his leg gave way.

Attempting to keep Billy off him, Grant lashed out wildly with both feet. But Billy was scrambling upright. He moved in a half circle, caught sight of Harmer with Grill and Delgado who were running towards the fight. He thought of Sarah Munnies and looked for her face, but took a moment too long. A ham-like fist thudded into his head, behind his ear. Another numbed his neck muscles and he felt his legs weaken.

Grant laughed nervously as he got to his feet, setting himself for some knockout blows. Billy blinked some sharpness back from a reeling blur, and drew his Colt. He held the frame flat in his hand, took one step forward and swung it hard. 'I need help,' he rasped, as the impact stabbed up his arm to his shoulder.

Grant was caught mid-stride. His eyes went out of focus before closing, and he collapsed like an off-loaded sack of potatoes.

'Get this dirt bag away from me, Harmer,' Billy managed.

The old-time sheriff grinned. 'I could've stopped this,' he rasped.

'Why the hell didn't you?'

'Because he's a pain in the butt an' needed to learn it, OK? Ike, you and Pinky take July back to the river, and wake him up.'

'Yeah, the cold water might shrivel his passion,' Delgado lifted his Derby an inch and chortled crudely in Sarah's direction.

Taking an arm each, Grill and Delgado dragged Grant to the water and dumped him in without ceremony. Face down, the man spluttered. He came alert instantly, turning over and thrashing wildly. Guffawing, using crude comments, the outlaws ringed him, pulling him to his feet. The beaten man weaved his way across the sand, started to remove his shirt before falling to his knees.

'I'd leave the girl alone if I was you, July,' Grill offered, walking past him moments later.

'You ain't me, goddamnit,' Grant spat the words down between his knees, into the sand. 'It's a question of time. You'll see.'

'Billy Newton might have somethin' to say about that,' Grill sneered. 'An' right now he's certainly a lot prettier.'

Billy held his soaked bandana against the nape of his aching neck. He saw the shadow approaching, turned and grinned. 'I hope we didn't disturb your bathe, ma'am,' he said.

'You make it sound like an infirmary treatment,' Sarah Munnies replied. 'My name's Sarah. I heard the others call you Newton? Is that your first name?'

'No, Billy. You sure chose a peculiar time for a dip.' Briefly stuck for words, Billy stared down at the bandana in his hand. 'There's cottonmouths in there. Close to the bank, too,' he said. 'Just stay where we can all see you.'

'I will. It seems I got caught between two nests of snakes.' Sarah countered, surprised by Billy's brusqueness.

Bigg Harmer broke the vocal wrangle. 'Mount up,' he announced, jerking the traps of the pack mule. 'We're going across.'

Eager to be on the move, the men grabbed for their horses. Sarah Munnies almost ignored Billy as

45

he gave her a leg up into the saddle. In turn, he couldn't understand what the young woman was so touchy about.

Ten minutes later the six riders were across the Whitewater river. Bigg Harmer was leading them further south into Mexico, towards Pelicano.

CHAPTER 4

Against the deep inky backdrop of night, firelight coloured the group's features. Forty miles into Mexico they sat intoxicated with fatigue, gripped by the small dancing flames. Pinky Grill threw more brush on the fire, then looked at Sarah. He lifted the coffee pot and knelt beside her. 'Coffee,' he said, and grinned, not unpleasantly. 'It won't do much good other than warm you up.'

'Leave her be,' Billy said.

Sarah lowered her dark, solemn eyes, but nearly smiled.

'What are you, Newton?' Grill asked. 'Her keeper? Her brother?'

Ike Delgado swallowed the last of his ribstick beans and turned his plate into the ground. 'Nothin' brotherly about him,' he snorted, holding out his tin mug. When Grill had filled it, he added to the coffee with something from his hip flask. 'Fact is, Pinky,' he continued, 'if you don't work your claim for a week, it's considered to be abandoned . . . reverts to public ownership.'

'Yeah, so I've heard.'

'An' what's good enough for a gold mine's good enough for us, eh Pinky?'

'Newton's obeying my orders,' Bigg Harmer interrupted, his face already showing the strain of their ride. Slumped against his saddle, the old lawman poked a bony finger at the contents of his plate.

'Oh yeah, your orders.' Delgado was beginning to feel the effects of his liquor. 'That's right, fellers. We got to sleep cold, 'cause sheriff decides who's pickin' our desert flower.'

'Like hell he does,' July Grant rasped through his broken mouth. 'No rusty badge-toter's goin' to shove me an' my pecker around.'

'You've just had someone do it to your face,' Harmer replied sharply.

The men looked towards the sheriff, saw the gleam from the twin barrels of the shotgun that appeared from under his blanket coat.

'That'll be one old gun against three,' Delgado said as he got to his feet.

Pinky Grill remained seated. His bald head shone, but his face was lost in shadow. 'You're not speakin' for me, Ike,' he said. 'You best make that two agin two.'

'You'll be standing with a loser, Delgado,' Billy joined in. 'Those aren't great odds. Especially when I toss *my* hat in.'

July Grant was angry and embarrassed. He accepted the situation by turning away and stomping into the silence of the night.

Ike Delgado sniffed, stared thoughtfully down at the coffee can he was still holding.

Watching him, Grill laughed. 'Not much interest in a fair fight, eh Ike?'

The outlaw curled his lip. 'Our sheriff's leadin' you around a goddamn rainbow,' he said. 'If he ain't got the money on him, it obviously don't exist. Can't you see? I'm bettin' as soon as we've finished his dirty work, he'll turn us in for whatever rewards he knows about.'

'Hell, got to admit it makes some sort o' sense.' Grill's face was hidden by shadows as he called out from across the dancing flames.

'You mean, some sort o' drivel,' Bigg Harmer said calmly. 'Soon as I settle with Quince, you owl hoots can choose any trail you like and how to spend your bounty. And that includes you, Ike.'

Grill pointed his 'Mule' at Delgado. 'If I was to shoot you Ike, I reckon you'd bleed horse crap,' the bald outlaw claimed. 'You figure killin' our sheriff would help? Goddamnit, that deputy of his knows more about us than our own kin.'

'Franklin Poole,' Delgado started. 'I forgot him.' The thin, bird-like man threw the can down in temper, followed July Grant away from the camp fire.

'Keep your ears pinned, Ikey,' Grill called after him. 'An' don't get lost. You wouldn't want to do us any favours.'

Harmer released the twin hammers of his shotgun and drew his blanket coat tighter around him. 'To think I'm paying him a thousand dollars,' he sighed.

'Aren't you going to eat those beans?' Sarah asked Billy.

'I hadn't reckoned on doing so, no,' Billy replied flatly.

'Wish I could sleep,' Pinky Grill commented with a glance into the darkness. 'Which way do we divvy up our sleep? Assumin' we're goin' to get some.'

'How about when Delgado comes in?' Billy replied. 'If that's what he's got in mind. I'll take the last four hours.'

'You trust me not to put bullets in you an' Harmer?'

'It's tiring not trusting anybody,' Billy said, and took a couple of steps towards Sarah. 'What are you staying awake for?' he asked.

With a thin, troubled smile, Sarah looked around her. 'Are you serious?' she replied.

'You'll be safe enough. Either me or Grill will be awake.'

'Thank you. That's reassuring. From what I heard, the whole bunch you have prices on your heads.'

'Well, that may be so. But there'll likely be a night critter . . . some old lobo that wants to take a bite at you. Suit yourself, though,' he said.

'I'm sorry . . . Billy. I wasn't thinking. I should have.'

'Yes, ma'am. It's unreasonable, considering one thing and another. Like the sheriff said, tomorrow won't be any easier. So keep the thought.'

Billy moved off a few paces, but on some sixth sense he stopped, hunkered down and drew his Colt. He rolled its chamber slowly across the top of his knee and watched the darkness, and thumbed back the action as July Grant walked into the fire-light.

Grant saw the Colt levelled at him, then the unmoving female form that shaped the blanket. The man had obviously been drinking, and sucked at the air in a loud nasal snort and spat. 'Gimme a town anytime. Anywhere but here,' he slurred. 'An' you can put that iron away, Newton. All I want to do's fall over.'

'Well you're headed in the right direction,' Billy replied. 'And if you're not asleep in five minutes, I'll slit your weasely throat.'

Grant's knees gave way and he folded to the ground. He concentrated on the weak shadows that outlined Sarah's sleeping figure, mumbled something, grinned and fell asleep.

Billy poked a stick around the embers of the

51

dying fire. The air was sharper now and carried wild scents from sweetbush and clover. The cry of a gray wolf carried from a distant timberline and he shuddered for a moment, and wondered if Sarah Munnies had heard it.

Billy pulled out his stem-winder and took note of the hour. Then he snapped the case shut and stepped around the embers. 'Your turn, feller,' he said quietly, shaking Pinky Grill awake.

Grill recognized Billy and kicked back the blanket. He lowered his gun, and shivered. 'That was a short night,' he complained. 'You did me a favour though. Missy wildcat was about to scratch my eyes out.'

'They say nothing's impossible in dreams.'

Grill took a quick look at the still, sleeping figures. 'Hmm. It *was* a dream, wasn't it?' he muttered. 'Anyone missing?'

'Only Delgado,' Billy said. 'He's out there supping with the wampus cat. Can I use your blanket?'

'Yeah. What's wrong with yours?'

'It's cold.'

'You mean someone else is snugged inside it.'

'I'll see you at first light,' Billy grated.

Grill kicked a tight clump of tumbleweed into the fire. As the embers spat and spluttered, Billy saw the man's hand grip his gleaming, short-barrelled rifle. He felt a curious touch of assurance and tugged his hat brim over his eyes. *Shut it*, he thought when a distant coyote gave another long howl.

A single shot crashed through the early morning air. It brought Billy to full alert and he cursed loudly as he scrambled to his feet.

Sarah Munnies reacted similarly, trying to square confusion with the reality in front of her. 'The sheriff,' she screamed. 'He's shot.'

Billy's mind was racing with the problem of who and why. 'Stay where you are,' he yelled at her. He actioned his Colt, and saw beyond the fire's ashes, where Bigg Harmer's knees were buckling. The man's tough hands were clasped to his chest and dark blood was already seeping through his fingers.

'The snake fed us a line o' bull crap,' Ike Delgado shrieked. 'The money's in his saddle-bags, like I said.'

Billy fired and Delgado gasped in pain as a bullet smashed his gun arm above the wrist. Billy walked quickly to Harmer, put an arm around him, easing him back to the support of his saddle. He undid a button of the old-timer's shirt and lifted back the sodden cloth. 'You'll have been hit worse,' he said, smiling encouragingly. 'Just don't eat too much.'

Billy gave Delgado a contemptuous glare. 'You've got another hand, you drunken scum,' he challenged. 'Use it to do something real stupid.'

'Never mind the heroics,' Pinky Grill snapped, prodding Billy with his big Mule gun. 'The same goes for all o' you, goddamnit.' The poker-faced outlaw reached out his left hand, grabbed Delgado and swung him roughly towards where Harmer's saddle-bags lay. 'Go on Ike, open 'em so's we can see what you're talking about. And you best come up with a few thousand dollars.'

'I'd like to see this trick,' July Grant joined in. He pushed the trembling, small-boned outlaw aside, scooped up the saddle-bags and emptied their contents on to the ground.

Continuing to shake the leather pouches angrily, Grant's eyes flashed from Delgado to Grill. 'Jerky,' he shouted. 'It's wads o' dried beef, an' this polecat's been proddin' us into a shootout with each other. Last night you might've killed us 'cause o' him, Pinky.'

'Yeah,' Grill nodded woodenly. 'I warned you what would happen if you tried to gull me again, Ike. I reckon Newton's got it right.'

Delgado gave a vigorous headshake. 'I got to thinkin', Pinky,' he wailed. 'That's why I came back in to help. I'm not goin' to raise a gun against you, an' you can't make me.'

'I don't want to make you, Ike. I want you to want to do it. You make me sick.' Grill took a step forward, levelled the barrel of his Mule at the cowering outlaw. 'This beauty could send that thick head o' yours half way back to the border.'

Delgado unbuckled his gunbelt, let it fall to the ground. 'I ain't armed, Pinky. Don't shoot,' he pleaded.

'He won't shoot you, Ike,' Grant sniggered. 'He's too mean, an' it's too quick. He wants to see you suffer.'

Backing off, Delgado looked around him. 'It was that double-crossin' deputy wanted Harmer dead. It weren't my idea,' he called out to them. Then he turned, and ran the short distance to the willow brake and instant cover.

'Hah, let's go get him,' Grant said, almost breaking into a run.

Sarah shivered at the cold, hard-bitten looks that glazed the eyes of Grill and Grant. 'For heaven's sake, stop them,' she pleaded to Billy.

But Billy was halted by Bigg Harmer's determined voice.

'Ain't a useful move, Newton. Without you, my chances of getting Tyler Quince will be that much slimmer.'

Facing the grey-faced lawman, Billy looked into the barrel of the old Colt that covered him, and cursed. 'What the hell's that for?' he flared. 'For chris'sake, if I hadn't lied on your behalf ... if they'd believed Delgado's story, you'd be floating down to the Gulf behind those pepper bellies.'

Harmer stared down at the spread of blood across his shirt. 'What was the lie you told 'em?' he asked.

'That you'd hidden the money somewhere along the border.'

'Weren't much of a lie,' the sheriff responded with a tired smile. 'But I misjudged our Frankie Poole,' he grunted, looking up to Billy's face. 'So I'm not that trusting of anyone at the moment. Why'd you do it, anyway?'

'You tell me,' Billy flipped back.

'What tree are you hacking at, Newton? Or what-ever your name is,' Harmer continued. 'My gut, such as it is, is telling me it's not the money. Some would say it's those Prescott lawmen, but I don't think you're that easy to scare. So what is it?'

'If I told. . . .' Billy started. He stopped as Harmer's grizzled chin sunk into the top of his chest and the Colt dropped from his fingers.

Billy looked around for Sarah. 'It's no more'n a flesh wound, but if you'll help, I could dig the lead out,' he declared. 'I've seen that sort o'stuff done to good bloodstock. It can't be that different.'

Sarah nodded, then started to consider what Billy would need to attempt such a procedure. 'Are you serious?' she asked uncertainly.

Opening up the sodden shirt again, Billy had a closer look at the dark red damage. 'No, not really,' he admitted.

'Then why'd you say it?'

'I thought I could finish what I was telling him.' Billy turned to Pinky Grill who had returned and wanted to take a closer look at Harmer. 'What's happened to Delgado?' she asked.

'Son-of-a-bitch must have fallen in and drowned,' Grill replied. 'God rest his soul.'

CHAPTER 5

'If he doesn't die, we take him with us,' Billy had said. And Harmer hadn't, and they did. With Ike Delgado's bullet lodged in his belly fat, the tough old lawman rode in front, hauling them on until full dark.

At dawn with his wound packed and strapped, he was first in the saddle. 'It's makin' itself at home,' he'd joked of the bullet to Sarah Munnie's concern. 'Hah. If all the lead inside me was gold nuggets, I'd retire to Dixie.'

Billy allowed Bigg Harmer new respect. He thought that Tyler Quince had even more reason to worry, but it didn't make his personal undertaking any easier. Somewhere ahead was the man he'd been hunting for two years, and he wanted him alive at all costs.

Harmer knew the country below the Whitewater. From previous ventures he'd learnt the hard way how the town of Pelicano could be approached in near secret.

'Not much further,' he said, shading his eyes. 'There's a river, an' that bench up ahead's where we can stop an' take a look.'

Billy reined in close. 'You sure Tyler Quince's there?' he asked.

The sheriff looked at Billy for a long moment before answering. 'This is the third time today you've asked me that. You sound as eager as me to meet up with him.'

'I want to be certain I'm earnin' my keep,' Billy lied. Together, the two men stared out across an immense stretch of dry, dusty badland, pale and hazed under a blistering sun. 'Besides, it's natural I'd be wondering where this caper ends, don't you think?'

Harmer took a pull from his canteen. 'I think there's not much wondering in my line of business,' he answered with a thin smile. Then he lowered his voice, turning to look back at the grim trio reining in behind. 'I owe you my life, son. Maybe twice over. But whatever purpose you got, it won't stop me taking you out if you get between my gun and Quince. You should know that,' he added with more bite.

Billy watched Pinky Grill drink with irritation from his canteen as he considered what the sheriff had said.

'We must've rode half way round the world. How

much goddamn further?' Grant whined.

'Maybe the sheriff don't know,' Grill offered, his face reddening where dust-caked beard didn't grow. 'Could be we're out sowin' sand. My patience is wearin' mighty thin.'

'Like mine,' Harmer retorted. 'Difference is, right now your opinion don't amount to a hill o' beans, Grill. Now, if you stop whingeing I'll show you where we're headed.'

The long, high-rising bench marked the end of the hostile land. Burning rock, spiny cactus and treacherous gopher holes were behind them. The horses climbed rapidly, and at the top, all but Bigg Harmer were suitably impressed at the landscape stretching below and before them.

'Hell,' Grant exclaimed. 'Is all that Mexico?'

'Yeah, twice bigger'n Texas,' Harmer said, dismounting slowly and removing his hat. He stood at the edge of a near two-hundred-foot drop, a rising breeze ruffling his iron-grey hair.

'And that's a town out there, is it?' Grill remarked.

'Pelicano,' Harmer replied.

'It don't look much of a place.'

'Unlike Walnut Bench.' Harmer nearly chuckled. 'It's deceptive . . . sort of reaches out.' Harmer threw a quick glance at Billy. 'Some paths lead to quarters you want to stay well clear of. Quince's spread is out of town aways . . . where the river's got a bow in it. It's kind o' weird, Tyler Quince wanting

60

something between himself and the town vermin.'

Grant was taken aback. 'He's got a spread? You never said he was a rancher.' The man's small, dull eyes blinked at a quick thought. 'Just how important is this feller?'

'Important enough,' Harmer said. 'I guess he could put a handful of pistolero guns on the payroll if he wanted to. So what?'

'So what?' Grant repeated incredulously. 'We could be goin' up against a small army! You forgot to mention that.'

'I didn't forget anything. For a thousand dollars, did you reckon on plugging fish in a barrel? You got to earn that sort o' cash.'

'We can take care of a handful,' Grill said. 'Greaseball guns'll die easy when me an' ol' Mule get angry.'

'Yeah, says you,' Grant snorted in reply. 'What's Quince done, Sheriff, that we should all risk dyin' for?'

'I already told you, I'm paying for the use of you and your gun . . . not giving the good cause. But if you want to know, Tyler Quince killed my daughter . . . suckered her here, then murdered her.' Harmer stared ahead, continued without obvious emotion or focus. 'His story was that she was drunk, fell off the balcony of some Mex dog hole and broke her neck. Huh. Raphy Rose never took anything stronger than lemon sumac.'

July Grant shifted awkwardly. Pinky Grill stared

thoughtfully across the land stretching south below them. 'Seems to me this Quince hombre's got some dues to pay,' he said, not much moved by what he'd just heard.

Billy turned towards the horses. 'How do we get down there?' he asked, feeling Harmer's eyes now on his back.

'I know an Apache trail that'll take us to the river. But hold up a tick,' Harmer said. The tough sheriff took a few painful strides, reached for Billy's arm and half turned him. 'You understand what I had to say . . . my beef?' he added, feeling the muscles in Billy's arm tighten.

'Yep. And I haven't forgot anything you've said.' Billy half smiled. 'It's a timely explanation, if you don't mind me saying so.'

Harmer released his horny grip and nodded. 'Guess I'm running on a short fuse,' he muttered, realizing what he'd done wasn't a good idea.

Billy looked at Sarah Munnies. 'She's earned a rest, Sheriff. Now seems as good time as any. What about it?'

'Not yet. Not until we hit the floor.' Without another word, Harmer swung cautiously back into the saddle. Focused once again, he headed a slow pace along the rim of the bench.

The wind serpentined through the stunted nut-pine trees that verged the narrow trail. For nearly an hour and in single file, the five riders with their pack mule alongside Ike Delgado's mount, dropped below the rim.

'Steady. You want to go following this stuff down?' Grill warned as rock chippings scattered under the horses' hoofs, falling a hundred feet to the floor.

'Good time for a big shot o' corn,' July Grant sniggered nervously.

Pinky Grill laughed. 'Mescal. It's good Mex liquor, an' I'll wager there's a 'dobe joint some-where down there just leakin' it.'

'You can forget all of that,' the sheriff's voice drifted along to them. 'We're riding wide of Pelicano. If I was Quince I'd have set me a watch-man or two in those likely places.'

Grant's face darkened. He fixed his eyes on the rider ahead of him, and in a fit of anger and frus-tration heeled his mount forward.

The trail wasn't wide enough to take two horses. Keeping to the inside, Grant held himself ready as the horses collided, shoulder against haunch. Seconds later, a startled squeal declared terror as the grullo mare was knocked off the trail.

Over Sarah Munnies' cry of horror, Grant yelled: 'Newton's gone. What the hell was he tryin' to do?'

'Haul in, goddamnit,' Bigg Harmer cursed, cursing more as he dismounted. He backtracked to where the horse and rider had fallen. He glowered at Grant, ground his teeth as he knelt and stared below.

'I don't know . . . didn't know what was happening,' Grant was muttering. 'Our horses went at each other for some reason. It could o' been me.'

Harmer turned towards Grant with a distrustful stare. 'But it wasn't,' he snarled. 'You got any idea what horse sense means? Give me your rope . . . quick.'

'Rope?' Grant looked dazed. 'What d'you want my rope for?'

'He's alive . . . here, thirty feet down. He's caught in the roots of some goddamn tree.'

Grant was hesitant, but the rasp of a rifle's breech action brought him to movement.

Pinky Grill raised the barrel of his Yellowboy. 'Get the rope, or you'll be deliverin' it personal,' he threatened.

Grant continued with his muttering as he unhooked his lariat and tossed it to Harmer.

'Billy. Can you hear me? I'm goin' to drop you a rope,' the sheriff yelled. 'Put your arm out, Billy. We can't come down with it.'

From where he was wedged, Billy could see the grullo far below, crumpled in a broken heap the way it had landed. He shook some sense back into his head, grunted and slowly raised an arm. 'This place has already got a visitor. Get me out of here,' he shouted back up the slope.

After a second and third attempt, the loose loop that Harmer had made draped around Billy's arm, dragging towards his shoulder.

64

Harmer immediately threw the slack end to Grant. 'Fasten it around your saddle horn.' His eyes blazed with suppressed anger. 'Tie it tight or I'll ask Grill to blow your legs off. You understand?'

Without another sound, the outlaw hitched the rope and Harmer shouted again.

'You've got to climb, Billy. I'm watching, but there's no one can pull you up 'cause the rock'll probably chew through the rope.'

Billy grunted a response. Thrusting both arms into the loop he took a deep breath and positioned himself to swing away from the stubby, gnarled branches.

The radiant heat mixed with anxious sweat made his hands slippery and he wasn't going to look down. The diamondback had started its warning rattle, but Billy guessed it wasn't about to strike out at him. If it did, it would end up on top of the grullo. Nevertheless he shivered at the thought before kicking his legs against the rocky face of the bench.

His short swing into open space seemed interminable, then his boots hit the face of the slope and he scrabbled for purchase. Not leaving time for footholds, he pulled and clawed upwards, using his feet, hands and arms until they were numb and near to useless.

'You made it,' Harmer gasped unnecessarily, holding out a token hand of assistance as Billy scrambled over and on to the narrow trail of the bench.

With his mind racing, Billy remained kneeling for a full minute before getting to his feet, looking cold-eyed at July Grant.

'Goddamn horses could've got us both killed,' the man offered. 'Thanks for bringin' the rope back.'

'I think you're a liar, Grant, and next time I won't bother with proving reasonable grounds,' Billy replied. Then he looked at the sheriff and nodded. 'I guess this makes us even,' he suggested.

Harmer shook his head. 'Call me pernickety, but I still owe you one.'

'Let's hope I don't have to call it in just yet. Meantime, I'll have to ride Delgado's dun.'

Harmer managed to return a thin smile. A short while ago he'd felt bad imagining Billy Newton dead. Into first dark, and he'd probably not even have seen any way of helping. Now, for reasons he couldn't be sure of, he felt good. 'Not much light left. Let's push along,' he barked, keeping any sentiment from his voice.

They descended to the flat land without further incident, working their way as close to Pelicano as the thickets of chaparral allowed. An hour later, using the dense cover and with the town in the near distance, the five riders dismounted.

Harmer studied the town and its reach. There was nothing specific, but he noted the many small dust clouds that coiled from the land.

'There's plenty movement out there,' he started.

'Looks like they're preparing for something. From here on in, no matter what we do, someone'll spot gringos. July, pull out those Mexican duds. It's the only way to get close. All o' you, 'cept Miss Munnies, o' course, get into the scrub and sort it out best you can. Reckon it's all a bit undersize, but the goddamn hats'll look the part. Soon as you're done, we'll get out o' these barrens. Anyone looks our way, they'll see Mexicans mixing with a few friendly gringos. Nothing too suspicious about that.'

Concealed by the chaparral, Billy stopped short of donning the tight, clammy trousers. If it took camouflage to get close enough to Quince he'd go with it, but there was a limit. Anyway, if anyone got to see some of them were only dressed as Mexicans, it would be gun time. He pulled on a heavy, suede jacket, tried not to recall the owner as he placed a high-crowned sombrero on his head.

With stress nipping away at his vitals, he took a few steadying breaths. In the hours ahead he would meet up with Tyler Quince, whom he wanted alive and talking. Somehow he had to keep him outside the gun range of Bigg Harmer.

Grant and Grill came walking towards him. Sporting their *vaquero* clothing and accessories, he hardly recognized them.

CHAPTER 6

Through the fine, rising dust, the low sun of late afternoon blurred the sight of the farmer. From the high seat of his carreta, with a child either side of him, he squinted against the tawny haze. 'Gringos,' he said. 'All of them,' he added uncertainly. He looked at the sombreros that marked out three of the five riders, and gave a tentative smile. He was thinking if they wanted to be perceived as Mexican, then that's how he'd politely speak to them. '*Buenos tardes, señors . . . señorita,*' he greeted.

But there was no response. The man shrugged, watched thoughtfully as the riders passed by. '*Estupido Americanos!*' he muttered.

'You hear the ol' chili?' July Grant sniggered. 'He thought we was real. You done some smart thinkin' there, Sheriff.'

'It's got me this far,' Harmer answered. 'Quince is wily, so *I've* got to be.'

Riding nearer to Billy, Harmer continued. 'From

the moment I found out the son-of-a-bitch was holed up here, I spent two days crawling around. I knew I was a sitting duck if he spotted me, though. Hell, there wasn't going to be much doubt what I wanted. From up on the rim, you can see thickets of scrub oak bordering his hacienda, so I waited for full dark. It's not close, but good for a rifle, and I figured I'd get a chance at him the following day. Huh, I was wrong about that. Those hired guns of his were gathered like hornets. Only someone with a real bad scare going keeps a bunch of hombres between him and the outside world.'

'All the time?' Billy queried.

Harmer laughed hollowly. 'Well, there's some places, but I couldn't get a sighting. And I'm not good enough to hit him from *everywhere*. If I missed killing him outright, his men would have taken me for nothing, and he'd have gone to ground some-place else.'

'And you reckon this is the best way?'

'Yeah, I reckon. We'll know shortly. Drop your chins,' he advised them all. 'I hear Mexicans sleep most of the time.' Leaving Pelicano behind them, the sheriff heeled his horse forward.

It was near first dark when they rode into the oaks that Harmer had talked about. 'We'll wait here until dark,' he said. The sheriff's pained eyes were brighter now, unblinking as he stared at the bleached adobe walls, just visible through the trees. 'Then we're going to ride in.' Tension had made his voice clipped and guttural.

Billy cautiously moved forward for a better look. Under the sun's last rays he peered at the big, two-storey house a hundred yards away. A high wall hid the ground floor, except where an open gateway gave him a glimpse of the hammered-earth court-yard, and a Mexican lighting up a *cigarito*. From a first-storey veranda, the polished steel of a rifle barrel flashed momentarily.

Harmer walked up and stood beside Billy. 'What do you think?' he asked quietly.

Billy considered. 'I think not all of us will be going home. But I'm also thinking we have an edge, in that they don't know we're here.'

Harmer said nothing. Preoccupied with their own hopes and fears, they stood side by side, watching the hacienda while the darkness pressed around them.

Full dark created a charged silence within the thicket. Billy and Bigg Harmer were still watching, peering beyond the lightning bugs, when lamps in the hacienda started to flare. Their light showed the location of some first-floor windows, but that was all, and the two men turned away.

Sarah Munnies was sitting apart from the outlaws, her face pale in the mean light. 'You're doing fine,' Billy told her. 'I can't imagine what it was you were headed for, but at least now you have a choice.'

'I know,' Sarah replied. 'But tell me about you.

You're not one of them . . . not even like them. So what are you doing here?'

On impulse, Billy hunkered down. 'Fair enough. I don't see much point in not telling you,' he said. 'I'm here because Harmer isn't the only one who wants Tyler Quince.' Seeing Sarah's bafflement, Billy took another direction. 'Quince is the one . . . the only person who can free me of a murder charge. That's many miles to the north of here, and about the long an' short of it.'

'I see. I think.'

'I hadn't figured on telling anyone that. If I thought there was a danger of you telling anyone, I'd have to . . .'

'Yes, I can imagine,' Sarah interrupted.

'It would be best for us both if you forgot what I just said.'

'Hey, I'm prescribing some gut settler,' came Harmer's timely interruption.

At the sight of the bottle being offered, the outlaws muttered incredulously.

'You're a hard man, Sheriff,' July Grant growled. 'I've been as dry as goddamn Death Valley all day long, an' there's *you* with a tit full o' cactus juice.'

'It's for medical purposes, and I've been waiting for the right moment. As I've said before, most things are about timing.' The old lawman's dry amusement sounded like far-away thunder. He drank and passed the flat bottle round. Billy didn't drink. He wanted nothing to dull any of his senses.

Grant received his share last, swallowed greedily, then pitched the empty bottle into the darkness.

'Christ, that's the way to finish a quart,' Harmer said. 'But this ain't high spirits of a carnival procession. We go in slow and quiet. Quince's looking for greasers with a pretty girl, so that's what we're giving him.' Turning to Sarah Munnies, the lawman continued. 'When we're inside that courtyard, you stay with the horses. Don't try and do anything else.' The sheriff concluded by speaking to the others. 'All of you remember, Tyler Quince is my kill.' He eyed Billy in particular for final emphasis. 'Mine and no one else's. OK – let's get it over with.'

Stars seeded the immense sky. Crossing a hundred yards of stark terrain, the silence played on their nerves. July Grant continually adjusted the gunbelt around his hips. Pinky Grill eased the stock of his Mule in its saddle holster. Somewhere ahead a dog picked up their scent and barked vigilantly. Harmer swore, because he hadn't considered the chances of that happening.

CHAPTER 7

'*Silencio . . . .bastardo, bestia.*' Calderon Pardo awoke, cursing from his sleep. Guilty at neglecting his duty, the guard was instantly into a startled, testy mood. 'Hijo de puta,' he added, but this time without the ironic smirk.

The dog was prowling the courtyard, slinking into the shadows, reappearing under light from a wall-hung brea lamp or window.

'*Nombre de dios.* What's up down there?' another guard called out from above.

Picking up his rifle, Pardo snorted out a reply. 'Take no notice. It's barking at shadows.'

'That's what it's supposed to do, *idiota.*'

The dog, now motionless and with its hackles raised, made a low, throaty growl.

'There's someone on the way in,' the second guard called out.

'*Sí*, more than one, I think.' Pardo levered a

round into the breech of his rifle and raised the barrel.

The five riders entering the gateway were now being watched as they rode into a wedge of weak light.

'Stupid dog,' Pardo scolded moments later. 'Zeke, Armando, Alfredo,' he called out, easing back the hammer. 'Senor Quince was just about to give up on you ever returning.'

The Mexican's dark eyes lingered on Sarah Munnies. 'Now, he will be pleased, *amigos. Muy complacedo.*'

When there was little in the way of a response, Pardo was unsettled. He looked even more closely at the riders, dread already twisting his sallowing features. The faces under the sombreros were unfamiliar, not even Mexican.

It dawned instantly on Pardo, why the dog had barked: it was warning him of approaching strangers. 'And there's one too many,' he whispered to himself.

'Gringos!' Fearfully, he yelled the reviled word. But it was only a second before Pinky Grill's Yellowboy Mule hammered his death blow.

'Everyone down,' Bigg Harmer shouted as bullets immediately spat holes into the ground around their feet.

Cursing and stumbling over Pardo's body, July Grant triggered a wild shot up at the guard who was firing from a corner of the first floor veranda. A bullet ripped across the top of his leg and he quickly dropped to one knee. 'If you want to play serious,' he warned, steadying his Colt in a two-fisted grip to fire. The guard shuddered, stared disbelievingly out into the night before roll-diving to the courtyard. His rifle clattered five or six feet from where Sarah Munnies crouched beside a massive clay urn. It was where Grant was retreating to, for his next cover.

Running in circles, the dog made chilling, whimpering noises around the Mexican's twitching body. From the base of the hacienda steps, Pinky Grill cursed and turned, his finger jerking once against Mule's trigger.

'Your loss, our goddamn gain,' he rasped icily, as the dog lay down beside its stilled master.

'Come on,' the sheriff yelled, lumbering past Grill, up the broad steps. He made it to the top, lunging awkwardly for the iron-bound doors as gunfire smashed out through windows. Behind them, a bullet ricocheted off the stone treads, then a water trough before zinging across the courtyard. 'Come on out, you lousy scum,' he yelled, having got to the door. 'You know who we're here for.'

Billy grabbed Sarah Munnies and ran her up against a front wall of the building. 'You'll be safer here. If they come out we'll deal with them,' he told her. But his voice betrayed a fitting uncertainty.

Harmer wanted Quince, and time was literally flashing away. Any one bullet from him or his men could mean two years of searching coming to an end, and for nothing. A dead man wasn't going to be made to understand where he'd gone wrong, the bad mistake he'd made.

Billy saw the glinting shards of glass that littered the courtyard as he followed Harmer and Grill up the steps. He cursed, and gritted his teeth as gunfire sounded again, but now it was from deep inside the *hacienda*.

'We're here, Quince, you scum-sucking pig.' It was the sheriff's voice that Billy recognized, echoing through darkened rooms and corridors.

Old fool, he thought, *hasn't sense enough to keep quiet even in the bear's den.* And Harmer's tirade wasn't answering the question of whether Tyler Quince was alive or dead.

Quickly considering the move the outlaws were taking, hearing the mighty blasts from Grill's rifle and the backup of Harmer's Colt, Billy turned away. He stalked along the veranda, ducking low alongside a line of closed glass doorways. Not a single light was visible from the rooms behind.

One of the doors appeared to be open a few inches, and what looked like a breeze from somewhere was gently pushing it open even more. Holding his Colt across his chest, Billy pressed himself against the pale adobe, and silently watched the spread of the long, slim wedge of darkness.

He edged a foot closer, then stopped, wiping sweat from his eyes with the crook of his arm. Then he stretched out his foot and kicked the door open.

Glass-shattered explosions shook the darkness. Orange flame spat once, twice, three times towards the veranda. Billy dashed into the room, went down and rolled in the sudden pitch blackness before a twin pair of shots added to the brief nightmare. He blinked, was certain he'd seen a ghoulish face, very pale and haggard behind the flashes.

'Quince? Hell, is that you, Quince?' he seethed breathlessly.

'No *señor. Un greaser con dos pistolas.*' The Mexican's words were cool and provoking, but they signed his death warrant.

In one rapid movement, Billy reached out and swiped his arm across a close-by tabletop. The contents flew across the room, a mess of flying papers and writing paraphernalia, drawing the expected fire. Over the writing table, Billy's Colt had a fleeting target, at another almost blinding flare of light he fired. He heard the body fall and fired again. He waited ten seconds, but the only sounds and movement were from another nearby place.

He stepped further into the room, almost dragging his feet so as not to trip over anything or anybody. He opened a door, using it to push aside the body, squeezing through into more interior darkness.

He was just about able to see by the light from a pair of ornate happy-jack lanterns at the end of the corridor. He avoided lifeless piles of clothing, sightless eyes, gaping mouths, jaws locked under the pall of smoke and acrid bite of cordite. The bodies were all Mexicans. 'They passed this way then,' he muttered bitingly, considering the whereabouts of Harmer and Grill.

He found them where the light from an oil lamp revealed the wholesale violence of their work, where shattered furniture and picture frames, adobe clumps and filthy Navaho rugs littered the floor. Pinky Grill was sprawled in a chair reloading the Mule, but his face was colourless and deathly. With glassy eyes he watched Billy walk past the lamp. 'Look after ol' Mule,' he grated and coughed thickly. He closed his eyes and slid from the chair, and Billy then noticed the dark, mortal wetness that soaked his shirt front.

'He did well ... would've earned his money,' Harmer muttered.

'Yeah. Him and his Mule,' Billy agreed. 'And Quince?'

'Nary a sign of him.' Harmer snorted dryly. 'You know what they say about them who fight and run away?'

'Maybe you were wrong. Maybe he was never here,' Billy suggested.

The sheriff shook his head. 'This is where he lives ... where he'll always return to. He just wasn't in.'

Billy gave a look of tired astonishment. 'Where then?' he asked.

'Maybe we'll find out.' Harmer pointed his big Colt at the wounded Mexican being shoved towards them by July Grant.

'Found him hidin' upstairs, shakin' an' a'shiverin' like a Thanksgivin' jelly,' the outlaw guffawed. 'Thought you could have some fun before I pop him.' Grant had caught a flesh wound, and his eyes were bright with a mixture of pain and excitement.

'On your knees, pepper gut,' he demanded.

'Cut it out,' Harmer rasped. 'This place must have some sort of liquor store. A *bodega*. Why don't you go find it?'

'That's more smart thinkin', Sheriff. I guess a good drink beats a good kill,' he said, a touch begrudged. 'But if he's not dead when I get back, he sure as hell will be shortly after.'

Harmer watched Grant go back into the corridor and stand outside for a moment, considering which way to go. Then he turned towards the fearful Mexican.

'*Ven aca*,' he ordered. The Mexican moved uncertainly, dark eyes flicking down to Harmer's Colt. The man seemed oblivious to the blood running from his own scalp, dripping from his ear.

'*Señor. Por favour.* Please don't kill me,' he pleaded kneeling, his blood quickly making dark shiny gobbets on the floor.

'I won't, but *he* will.' Harmer nodded towards Billy. 'The dead man here was his best buddy,' he lied. 'Or I could leave you for when July returns. Both nasty ways to go, believe me. So, you tell me where Señor Tyler Quince is, and I'll see you live.'

The Mexican came up with the information immediately. 'He is in Pelicano with his *compañeros*. They are at the corn fiesta. Can I go now?'

'No, you stay here. But you live,' Billy assured him.

Moments later, July Grant reappeared in the doorway, carrying a wine bottle. 'There's a goddamn cellar,' he started, leering at the prisoner. 'I thought I said . . .'

'Never mind what you said,' Harmer cut in. 'Just tie him up. Lock him in a cupboard somewhere. We're going to a party.'

Grant lifted the bottle and shouted. 'Like hell we are. I've found me a place where all drinks are on the house.'

'And I've found Quince. He's in Pelicano,' Harmer replied. 'That's what I'm paying you for. Not staying here and getting blind drunk.'

'You ain't paid me nothin' yet, goddamnit. We done the bit we're supposed to be gettin' paid for.' Grant pointed towards Pinky Grill. 'Not that it did him or Ike much good. So, you get me my share, Sheriff, an' I'll think on it. Maybe even stand you a drink in the town when it's over.'

Harmer hefted his big Colt. 'Get the horses or you'll regret this,' he warned.

Billy thought this was the diversion he needed, and had moved nearer the doors that led to the courtyard. If Tyler Quince was in Pelicano, there was no reason for him to stay listening to the incendiary exchange between Harmer and Grant.

'We've been up to here with you an' your lousy orders, Harmer. If you want to make an issue of it, I'll goddamn oblige you now,' Grant continued, and clawed for his holster.

Harmer was almost ready for the move. He fired first, but he hadn't taken aim.

The bullet ripped past Grant's neck. Cursing, he dropped the bottle and threw himself sideways. He fired in return, but instead of hitting Harmer, his bullet caught the Mexican who was stumbling back to his feet. The man gasped in pain, clutched his shoulder, trying not to go back down again.

The sheriff pulled over a table, propped his Colt and snapped a shot back at Grant. The outlaw's legs trembled, and he slipped on shards of broken glass as he attempted to get to the inner door. But Harmer's bullets stopped him and he fell to the shelter of a hide-covered chesterfield. Two more bullets ripped into the couch's stuffing, but with Harmer's gun trained on him it was too dangerous for Grant to return fire. From his knees, he reached for the standing lantern, and in one movement heaved it in an arc up and near towards where Harmer was standing.

The lamp broke just beyond the sheriff, instantly spreading oil across the boarded floor and into scuffed rugs. It caught the hem of a heavy curtain, and orange flames licked hungrily upwards.

'For God's sake, Billy, shoot the son-of-a-bitch,' Harmer yelled – but in the same instant realizing he'd been left behind.

Taking advantage, and thinking he had to keep Harmer away from Grill's Yellowboy, Grant raised his head above the sofa and fired two more shots directly into the table. 'Now I'll be wantin' a portion o' Pinky an' Ike's share, goddamn you,' he shouted angrily. 'You're on your own, badge-toter.' He hunkered back down, reloaded his Colt, yelping near manic laughter. 'If you don't get out o' here soon, you'll be beef biscuit.'

The tough old lawman felt the pressing heat behind him. The flames eating into the surrounding woodwork were now lighting up the room. Seconds from now he would be forced to move, and when he did he'd be shot down like the rest of his bogus posse.

But then, through the flames of the smoke-filled room, a figure was suddenly shadow-dancing on the wall opposite. Harmer gaped disbelievingly. The man was shrouded in the deep orange glow, his gun firing steadily at the sofa where July Grant had raised himself up.

Harmer watched almost fascinated as Grant twisted towards him, a cheerless, puzzled smile warping his features. The Colt slipped from the man's grip and blood oozed from his mouth. He regained control of his Colt, in a final despairing gesture hurled it a few feet in Harmer's direction. Then he turned and staggered, reached out and dragged the flaming drapes down on top of him.

An eager, crackling fire was now filling the room, and burning debris blasted sparks upwards to the ceiling.

'Son-of-a-bitch tried to kill me,' Billy rasped. 'He was never going to learn.'

Billy took Harmer by the arm, drawing him towards the doors that led out on to the courtyard. Coughing and blinking hard, the lawman looked back into the raging fire. He was wondering about the Mexican, assumed he'd escaped just as they had done. 'Fighting wages don't always mean much,' he muttered grimly.

'Grant's dead. Along with Delgado and Grill,' Billy told him. 'Now it's just you and me.'

Sarah Munnies gasped nervously as the two men staggered into the starlight. Behind them, thick smoke had started to roll and billow through the rooms and hallways of Tyler Quince's *hacienda*.

Almost immediately they were outside, Billy reached for Delgado's horse and swung himself into the saddle. He made reassuring noises, and eased the dun mare alongside Sarah.

Her dark eyes reflected the burning hacienda as she stared at him fearfully. 'What's happening?'

'We're not staying, is what's happening,' Billy shouted. 'If Quince spots this fire when the roof goes up, he won't be thinking it's an early sunrise. He'll ride.'

'Yeah,' Harmer agreed, jigging awkwardly to find a stirrup on his own horse. 'He'll head straight from town . . . any road except the one back here.' The sheriff pulled himself into his saddle. He dug his heels impatiently, and without another word, rode for the *hacienda*'s gateway.

Knowing Sarah was a skilled rider, Billy smacked a fist into her mount's rump. 'Back through the trees,' he yelled. 'You'll be wide of me and Harmer.'

Billy could soon see Sarah's light capote ghosting against the night as he trailed her in and out of the oak thickets. At the same time, Harmer was already a quarter mile ahead, riding hell for leather towards Pelicano.

Ten minutes later, a deep scarlet glow lit the flat country. Billy turned in his saddle, took a final glance at what was now a funeral pyre for maybe ten Mexican *vaqueros* and two American outlaws.

CHAPTER 8

Under the stars, Billy just about kept Bigg Harmer in sight. Ahead of them and glimmering in the darkness was their goal, Pelicano. Somewhere near was a big, dark-haired man who dressed fancy and was partial to women and gambling. Tyler Quince was also a liar and a killer.

Riding steady, Billy caught up with Harmer on the western outskirts of town. The sheriff's mount was at a standstill, sweat-lathered and breathing like a steam engine. Seeing Billy approaching, Harmer flicked the reins and kicked the horse's flank. It drew a big snort, but that was all.

Slewing his dun to a standstill, Billy grinned humourlessly. 'Having trouble here, Sheriff?'

Harmer kicked free of the stirrups. 'Yeah. We're both all in.' Harmer swung heavily to the ground and stumbled. 'I guess this belly shot's taken more out of me than I thought,' he rasped. For a second he turned his back on Billy, a dark silhouette before the glint of Pelicano's lights.

'Are you OK? What's going on?' Billy asked.

The lawman turned back fast. 'Just this,' he said, having drawn his Colt. 'Get down.' Then he gasped when he saw that Billy already had the drop on him.

'You've pointed that goddamn smoke pole at me once too often, you old goat,' Billy replied. 'So put it away, unless you're going to use it.'

Harmer kept his old Colt levelled. 'Words ain't ever fazed me much, young feller.' Casting his eyes towards the horizon, he cursed. 'You can see that red glow from here, so why can't Quince?'

'He probably can. Or will shortly. Then what do you think he'll do? Ride out to investigate with fire buckets?'

'I think he'll know I'm real close. So I don't want you messing up or getting in the way. I'm guessing I had to stop you. Or try.'

'I could say the same about you, Sheriff,' Billy snapped back.

'Stop me? Yeah, we never did get to figuring out who you really were, Billy Newton . . . what you're wanting to be here for.'

Billy didn't respond, just stared poker-faced at the sheriff. A mutual respect made both men reluctant to start shooting. Yet within the next few minutes, they knew they would have to exchange bullets if one of them didn't back down.

'Quince murdered my daughter,' Harmer said with urgent feeling. 'That's what gives *me* the right to make it even.'

Billy's expression was colder now. 'She'll be avenged at the end of a rope. Somewhere between here and Big China Wash.'

'Huh. Now I know it was you shot the rancher a couple of years ago.' Harmer wiped the back of his left hand across his eyes. 'Perhaps you haven't got the stomach for summary justice. Is that it, Newton . . . or should I say Finch?'

'Whatever, Sheriff. To all of it. You'll abide by that star of yours when the time comes, but I'm not carrying the same consideration.'

'I was a father before I was a sheriff, mister. So now we know the set of things, you can get out of my way.'

'Can't do, Sheriff. And you owe me, remember? It's time for me to call in the debt.'

Harmer's weather-beaten forehead crinkled with uncertainty. 'Reckon I hurt too much for goddamn etiquette,' he grated.

Billy was faltering too, with his two-year reckoning plan suddenly defied by Harmer's visceral justice. He was about to give a final ultimatum when the dilemma was interrupted. Glancing quickly at the sheriff, he turned his head at the sound of approaching hoof-beats. It was from the blue darkness of the swing trail he'd told Sarah Munnies to take.

Billy quickly swung down from his saddle, took a couple of steps and reached out for the horse's bridle. 'Your tough break's turned up, Harmer,' he said, dragging Sarah's eager horse to a halt. 'She's *your* responsibility, remember?' Then in answer to Sarah's obvious bewilderment: 'This is as near as you're getting to town, tonight,' he said. 'Sheriff's horse sees it that way too. It's not quite the way I'd planned it, but alternative plans are sometimes for the better. Maybe one day you'll thank me,' he added with a weak smile.

'You ever going to tell me why you're here?' Harmer cut in.

Billy climbed back on the dun. 'Yeah, later, Sheriff,' he said. 'If things go wrong and I'm not back here an hour before sun-up, take Sarah back across the border. Evening,' he added and touched the brim of his hat.

After nearly five minutes of thoughtful silence, Sarah looked at Harmer. 'He's gone after Quince, hasn't he?' she said.

'Yes, he has. And he knew I couldn't help him. But he'll be back.'

Harmer and Sarah stared at the sprawl of the distant town. Faint, discordant sounds drifted to them on a cool breeze.

'They call it "fiesta". They're always celebratin' somethin' at sometime,' Harmer said, and sighed. All at once he felt old and weary, that he'd lost his edge – like a silver dollar too long in circulation.

Billy's mare shied away from the sounds of the fire-crackers. Dark shadowy faces stared up at him, even

88

those of young children who flashed laughter at the apparent response to fear. Jokey derision rose shrilly as they watched his hand waver close to the butt of his Navy Colt. They were still shouting after him as he rode on.

Halfway along the main street, at the town's crossroads, another crowd was gathered, a group of simply dressed townsfolk, each waving a yellow kerchief or small flag that represented a bountiful maize crop. A large pinwheel on a pole changed its glittering sparks from silver to gold, signifying a full, ripening sun. As the wheel stopped spinning it hung with its spent curls trailing lazily above their heads. The dance slowed in anticipation until the next colourful sunburst, when the guitars and trumpets picked up again.

'*Viva fiesta!*' a drunken peon shouted, and Billy nodded. Quince's *hacienda*'s having a display tonight, he thought dourly, heeling the mare slowly through the crossroads.

'Hey, gringo man,' another voice called out to him.

Billy reined in, and looked up to see another Mexican standing atop the wooden staircase of a grain store.

The man grinned. 'You a friend of Señor Quince,' he said.

Billy grinned back, his muscles tightening. He wasn't sure if the man was asking or making a simple statement. 'Si, amigo. I think I might have lost him somewhere in the maize field here,' he risked with a tentative smile.

A cackling laugh shook the Mexican. 'Then look for the prettiest *señorita* in Pelicano . . . the *niña bonita*. Find her and. . . .'

Yeah, makes sense. That, and a handful of cards, Billy thought. '*Gracias,*' he said, and swung towards the cantina directly opposite. He hitched the mare to the rail, ducked under the hanging veranda, and peered above batwing doors into a murky, smoke-filled bar room. Surrounded by an encouraging crowd, a piano player was banging out a fast, cockroach rhythm. They were all watching a girl with pitch-black hair who was smacking her hands like castanets and stamping tight-fitting boots along a low bench.

He studied the faces lit by the spluttering oil lamps, but Quince wasn't there. He would have stood head and shoulders above most of them if he had been.

Billy walked on, but there was no sign of the man. There were several what appeared to be cantinas or tequila taverns. 'How the hell many more are there?' he muttered. He saw a few swarthy figures lurking in shadows and doorways. Nearly all noticed his passing by, acknowledging him with a perceptible nod.

He pushed against the weighty oak door of the church, scanned the aisle, the few rows of dark wood benches. It wouldn't be the first time a sinner had taken to hiding in a blessed sanctuary. But again it was a fruitless search, and Billy had wasted a half hour. He went back and picked up the mare, and rode back to the town crossroads.

The crowd had actually grown in size and the sound was loud and more raucous. The mare walked forward against a mass of people who were hopping and skipping to the strains of the mariachi street band. Hands grasped at Billy's legs, for some reason tried to drag him from the saddle.

'Fiesta is no horses. No *caballos*,' one old man observed loudly.

Struggling to keep seated, Billy's eyes swept angrily over the crowd. He saw a large, taller figure among them, a face whose half-drunken eyes met his above the network of partying, yelling Mexicans.

Billy cursed and kicked the mare hard. People scrambled aside, and those who didn't were almost trodden underfoot. Scraps of street food, a wine bottle whistled through the air. Bending low, Billy kept the dun moving, shoving its way towards the tall figure who was backing off to the steps of a hardware store.

The man who'd stood on the staircase had been right. The *señorita* clinging to Tyler Quince's arm was indeed beautiful, but as of the moment, might not have existed. As Billy weaved towards them, Quince violently shoved her away, cursed fearfully and went for get-away and survival.

Rushing up the steps, Quince brushed aside his

long waistcoat and grabbed a Walker Colt. He turned and fired on the run, and a man in the milling crowd silently threw up his arms.

'Meet your real Tyler Quince,' Billy yelled, as abuse was screamed after him.

Quince fired off two more shots, but exploding fireworks jumbled the noise. The bullets were high, burying into adobe walls as he got nearer to the building where he hoped to lose his pursuer.

The steps met a log-covered veranda that extended nearly the whole of one side of the square. Quince stumbled as he frantically ran to get out of sight, colliding with a table and sending its occupants reeling, plates, glasses and bottles flying.

Scrambling to his feet a villager cursed Quince, but moments later waved an impotent fist at the horse and rider who chased close behind. '*Dos Americanos*,' he exclaimed. '*Dos diablos!*'

Billy had ridden straight up the front steps, then a hundred feet along the simple boardwalk.

Quince turned and sent back stabs of red flame. Bullets pulsated close to Billy but he couldn't return the fire. A missed shot might easily have killed an innocent reveller.

Leaping the gap between two buildings, Quince ran for the open side entrance to a carpenter's shop. Simultaneously, a joyful cheer rose up from the square as another string of bright fireworks cracked the night.

The dun mare responded sharply as Billy hauled

on the reins when he reached the deep darkness of the open doorway. Nervous and keeping his Colt pointing into the gloom, Billy slid from the saddle. Quince could be waiting just inside the doorway or looking for a rear exit.

Billy wiped the crook of his arm across his face, felt the run of sweat between his shoulder blades. Then pushing the mare aside he smashed the frame of his Colt against the side of the building. Thinking the sudden noise would alarm Quince by briefly taking his mind off the doorway, he rushed in, spinning to one side as he entered.

He dropped to a crouch, arcing the darkness with the actioned Colt. But he sensed there was no one there, and he was wasting valuable seconds while Quince used the time to escape.

Adjusting to the darkness, Billy's eyes located the only other exit from the workshop. Partly opened, a rear door gave access to a supplies yard.

Not wanting to go any further into risky, unfamiliar territory, he turned back and faced the square. Now the crowd was thinning out, most of the townsfolk realizing there was something more going on than fiesta celebrations. A few drunks and misfits were wandering around, mostly up to no good, but doing no real harm either. Billy grabbed the reins of his mare, considered where Quince would likely head to. *If he had any sense he'd run for the corral, or wherever it was he'd hitched his horse,* he thought. *Either that, or he's watching me right now.*

As if in response to what Billy was thinking, someone shouted angrily.

'*Quien? Quien esta?*' the voice called out, and Billy cursed as he swung round. He guessed that Quince had been lying in wait in a passageway behind him, and had probably trodden on someone in the darkness.

'Stay here,' Billy told the mare when he saw something move. Too fleeting for identification, the shadow melted into the darkness and disappeared. Billy ran straight for the alley, peering ahead for another movement, then took a few more cautious steps, straining his senses against the background noise to see and hear.

The mild breeze carried the stink of stable manure and rotting garbage. Billy puffed out his cheeks and looked to the stars twinkling overhead, wondered if he was heading for the town's market dump. *Maybe the whiff of a frightened Quince,* he mused icily on the man he was stalking.

A metallic gleam caught his attention and he knelt to pick up two spent cartridges, making a wry smile at the thought of Quince stopping to reload. *Yeah, I'm following, an' you've got a fully loaded gun,* he thought.

Billy felt the clamminess of unease against his body and expelled his held breath. He backed out of the narrow passageway and turned to look across the square. A fountain bubbled dark water, and discarded papier-mâché masks floated around its base.

94

He looked for shadows in and around the depleted taco and fruit stalls, and slowly walked towards his mare.

The dun kicked agitatedly at the dust, lifted its head and turned an eye in Billy's direction. The notes of a solo guitar drifted across the square. It underscored the unfolding drama, and Billy started at a suspended honeymelon swaying on a meat hook; in the darkness and shadow it was the right height to look like a human face, almost enough to make Billy fire. He circled a poled stall, looked at some of the merchandise that had been left on display – ponchos, hats, hanging pots. The place was a nightmare of forms that could trick you in the darkness. As far as Billy was concerned, it would take the morning's early sunlight and a throng of people to make it safer.

CHAPTER 9

The honeymelon exploded in a colourless cloud of mush and seeds. Billy dropped into a crouch, his ears ringing with the blast of Quince's Colt. Red flame blossomed again from the end of a short line of stalls.

A bullet smashed through the melon a second time, and Billy caught a spit of juice across his face. Three more shots followed closely and he doubled up and waited.

Quince had one remaining bullet, and before he reloaded, Billy knew he had to make his move. He wondered wryly where the one bullet could likely hit him, what the odds were of it being one of his vital organs.

'Hell,' he muttered crisply, gulped a breath and leaped for a space beside an adjacent food stall. He saw the gun flash and heard, saw where the bullet ripped through a side flap. 'Now it's my turn,' he rasped. Stooping below a line of trestle tables he kept very still and listened intently.

He heard the sound, the unmistakeable click of a Colt's rotating chamber. Quince was reloading, so he had to make his move. He ran directly to the end of the line of tables and shoved his own Colt out in front of him. 'Got you, you son-of-a-bitch,' he snarled. 'Drop the gun.'

Quince stared helplessly at the open chamber, up at Billy, then let the revolver fall from his grip.

Billy took a step forwards. He picked up the Walker Colt and stuffed it into the back of his trousers' belt. With the barrel of his own Colt, he lifted the brim of Quince's hat, looked hard into the man's angry eyes. 'Last time I did this it was the wrong man,' he said. 'I'm not making the same mistake again, Quince. Get up. Running away didn't work.'

Stepping backwards, Quince stared defiantly around the empty square. 'It would've done but for you, goddamnit. Pancho . . . *Perro* . . . !' he shouted, 'Where in hell are you?'

'Shut up,' Billy warned. 'We're leaving.'

'Leaving? Where to?'

'Prescott. But Walnut Bench before that. And the ride back's going to be a longer one than we all took to get here.'

'Your brain must've leaked,' the big man protested, looking over Billy's shoulder. His eyes were switching expectantly from side to side, trying to take in detail or movement from the dark, shadowy surroundings.

'But call out again, and all that changes,' Billy rasped. 'Certainly for you.'

'Huh, you've already said it,' Quince responded quickly. 'This is all about you needing me in one piece, Finch. I'm staying here.'

'I only need you alive, not unmarked and not necessarily whole, you cowardly scum.' Billy almost spat the angry words. His Colt moved, roared, and a gobbet of hard dust puckered a couple of inches from Quince's left foot. 'Hard to ride with half a foot, but you will,' he threatened. 'Now move . . . the street opposite the fountain. Remember, I can just as easy put a bullet into you somewhere else.'

Accepting the real threat in Billy's voice, Quince started to walk. Beyond the fountain he looked anxiously at dark windows and doorways, along the low, flat rooftops.

'Oh, they're there . . . can probably see you, but they don't care,' Billy said. 'They're probably thinking "*buen salida*", or something similar.'

'How'd you find me?' Quince asked.

'I joined a posse. How else?'

'What do you mean, a posse?'

'Harmer's riders. You remember Bigg Harmer . . . his daughter? What was her name . . . Rose?'

Quince stopped walking and half turned. 'Hell. You get Harmer involved in this an' we won't get further'n the end of the street.'

'Yeah, we will. We've got an arrangement, and

98

he's waiting up right now.' As he spoke, Billy saw a shadowy figure drift into view up ahead. Then closer, another detached itself from a doorway. 'Looks like I might have been wrong about your pistoleros,' he added, quiet and rueful. He glanced behind him, and his vitals trembled. At the fountain, one of them was spurting water after taking a drink from the chained tin mug.

'Three of 'em,' Billy muttered tonelessly.

Quince had also seen them and gulped with relief. 'My boys,' he said smugly. 'Hand me my gun and you'll live that much longer.'

Billy shoved the barrel of his Navy Colt hard into Quince's kidneys. 'I'm real short on Pelicano,' he whispered roughly. 'I'm getting out, one way or another.'

Displaying rictus grins under their sombreros, the three *pistoleros* quickened their approach. But the darkness presented them with a problem. Billy was garbed partly in the clothes of one of their own, but they also saw the drawn Navy Colt. They got wary and suspicious and very uncertain about him. The one in front held out a gloved hand. 'Hey, *amigo*,' he started, '*Qué pesando?*'

Billy knew the outward sociability was disguising a malicious intent. He also knew it was a curious protocol that associated self-defence with second dabs. He shrugged, half smiled and lowered his Colt. It looked like he was responding to the deceit of Quince's gunnies, and with widening grins the

Mexican trio got a few steps nearer.

But Billy wasn't considering an exchange of words or any codes of behaviour. He had an alternative tactic. In a fast, controlled movement he lifted the barrel of his Colt towards the first man and fired. Then he moved to the second and fired again. As both men fell, he fired second bullets at both. Four shots in four seconds was significant, but his life had been on the line and it made the difference.

He pulled a dazed Quince into a doorway and watched as the Mexicans died, face down and less than six feet from each other. The third man was confused between returning fire and running for cover.

Billy took aim, but didn't pull the trigger. He wasn't about to kill unnecessarily. 'I'm banking on you not paying 'em loyalty wages, Quince,' he rasped. 'Come daybreak, he'll be at the California Gulf.'

'But *they* won't,' Quince replied.

Billy followed the man's gaze to see four or five men coming fast from the other direction. 'Hell, I thought you'd hired proficient guns, not armed goat herds,' he said derisively. 'Back off or I'll shoot your paymaster,' he shouted. 'The *pagador*. I'll bet he hasn't paid you up front.'

The gun-carrying group hesitated, and Quince yelled after Billy's warning. 'He's lying, *amigos*. Shoot him.'

Billy cursed and slapped Quince aside. He grasped the door's iron handle, twisted it viciously and it turned to open. Grabbing a fistful of Quince's coat in his left hand he stumbled into the dark interior, kicking the door shut as he heaved the man to one side. A fusillade of bullets immediately hammered against the oak planks. On its old hinges the door broke open and gunsmoke drifted slowly in from the street.

Keeping Quince in front of him, but to one side of the doorway, Billy backed up until he was against a rear wall. The building seemed to be deserted, no persons, stores or furniture, and nothing or nobody had moved outside.

The darker shadow of someone came into view, and Billy fired his remaining bullet. He felt for the gun tucked into his trouser belt, then started to quickly reload his own Colt. Thumbing open the chamber, he levered five cartridges on to the floor and reloaded with live ones.

'Give it up, Finch, or we'll both end up in this town's bone yard,' Quince said.

'Still yellow to the centre, eh Quince?' Billy replied. 'Better though. I was wondering about your liking to chew the ol' dog.'

With his left hand, Billy ran his fingers along and across the wall behind him. He located a door latch, and lifted it. The door opened away from him, and he stood for a second listening intently. But whatever the room was used for, it was just as empty.

'Get over here. We're leaving,' he commanded.

Having pushed Quince through the doorway, Billy followed so close that his Colt was pressed hard against the man's spine.

There was a dog-leg alley that bent back to the main street. Billy could tell from the noise that more groups were continuing the festivities close by. 'That'll do us, eh Quince?' he said. 'Safety in numbers among women and children.'

Keeping his head lowered, he shoved Quince forwards into the crowd. He saw two *pistoleros* walking from the front of the building they'd just been in and out of. 'Yeah, like Harmer says, it's about timing,' he muttered in some relief.

One of the two Mexicans spotted Billy and Quince immediately. He said something and pointed the end of a cigarito in their direction. His companion raised the glinting barrel of a rifle, but decided against firing. Instead, he waved it across the street.

Looking to see whereabouts, Billy saw another rifleman on a rooftop, dark against even darker sky.

'They've got you tree'd. No way left but down,' Quince chuckled.

'That'll be you and me, both,' Billy said and pushed Quince further into the lively street. He considered how a stove-up old sheriff and a virtually bound girl could maybe be of considerable help. And where would the mare have wandered off to?

Turning Quince along the street, they were nearly outside the building they entered only minutes previous. Two pistoleros were taken by surprise, their jaws dropping, dark eyes blinking rapidly in confusion. They couldn't understand how they had suddenly becoming the hunted. They didn't even consider the guns they carried.

Realizing there was no way out, Billy shook his head, and fired.

The lead smashed into the first man's belly. He took a step forward, turned to his colleague imploringly and dropped his rifle. He looked at Billy and collapsed. Slumping into a sitting position against the wall, it looked like he was smiling at the bright insanity of the fiesta.

Billy had no choice but to fire again.

The second pistolero saw Tyler Quince and shouted a Spanish curse. He managed to squeeze a shot into the ground, before two bullets punched him hard in the chest. He only had time to look down at the blood before dying, keeling over sideways to the hard-packed dirt of the street.

Billy slapped Quince with the Colt, nudged him in the back to move him.

Half turning, Quince ranted: 'You're a killer, Finch.'

'I only ever wanted you, Quince. *You* to tell the truth about what happened. This is your hell hole . . . your making, not mine.'

'An' now Harmer's going to kill *me*. What's the

point then?'

'He won't kill you. You're going to hang.'

Billy stepped around the bodies, looked up and smiled in relief when he saw his mare. It was standing at the fountain with its neck bowed and ears pricked.

'This isn't where I left you, goddamnit,' Billy scolded amiably. 'We'll have to see about short rations.'

Billy mounted, and dragged his captive up behind him. 'Make a move I don't like the feel of and you won't have to worry about Harmer killing you,' he threatened.

Heeling the dun gently, he reined across the near-deserted square, skirted the stalls and entered a long, wider lane that ran parallel to the main street. He walked past the batwing doors of a cantina, heard the music of the guitar that was playing earlier. He drew out his stem-winder and held it close to see the time. He grunted, snapped the case shut and put it back in his pocket.

Parallel to where the church lay in the main street, he drew rein. Hoof-beats drummed nearby, sounding like a handful of determined riders.

'Yeah, I hear 'em too,' Quince said. 'Some o' those you've shot dead, might be their kin.'

Billy didn't say anything, just urged the mare into a gallop. They left the outskirts of the town, ran into quiet, open darkness beyond the maize fields. Carrying double, the horse began to falter after five minutes, snorting and stumbling as it veered close to a stand of tall yuccas.

'Billy? Is that you, Billy?' the voice of Bigg Harmer called out.

'You better hope so,' Billy replied, already sensing the increased tremor from Tyler Quince. 'I've brought the prize out with me,' he added, pulling in beside the shadowy figures waiting for him.

Harmer stared with revulsion at Quince. 'You really brought me the murderin' son-of-a-bitch!' he seethed, his pent-up feelings clearly determining his next move.

'Don't,' Billy warned, placing the palm of his hand on his Colt. 'I didn't gunfight half of Mexico to end up with a corpse. Besides, we got company,' he added, indicating over his shoulder, with a sideways nod.

Harmer continued to rage inwardly while he listened out. 'Sounds like a bigger army than what I've got. His men? His rats?'

'Yeah.' Billy offered a small, hopeful smile towards Sarah Munnies, who was sitting quiet and nervy. 'Let's give 'em a surprise ride. They must know we're hereabouts,' he said.

Harmer pulled his rifle from its saddle scabbard, levered a shell into the breech and sent a single shot out across the desert. It was a signal of defiance, a gesture not to follow. 'This old puddin' foot won't hold with a fast run,' he said. 'But there's a dried-up wash, runs to the west, an' it's close by. We get there, chances are we'll lose 'em.'

Billy nodded 'Suits us. Lead the way.'

Another half mile of difficult riding and they broke trail, swung through more high yucca, and walked down into a mesquite-choked, flat-bottomed gully.

'At least these beasts of burden will stay quiet for a while,' Billy muttered, more to himself than anyone else. Quince was staring up above the steep sides of the gully towards the dark skyline, away from the blinkless gaze of Bigg Harmer.

'It's all down to you, you scum,' Harmer whispered hoarsely. 'If we don't get out of here, at least *you* won't know it.'

After what seemed like an eternity, the hoofbeats of the approaching riders were a dulled tattoo on the hard-baked earth. Harmer, Sarah and Billy held their horses in check. Above them, the Mexicans didn't slow down, and in a short while the distinctive shapes of their sombreros had disappeared along the higher trail.

Within seconds, Harmer rounded on Billy. 'Now, give me good reason why I'm not shooting this rat?' he started with husky emotion. 'It's going to be the same end game.'

'You're a lawman for a start,' Billy said. 'I'll tell you quickly why: I'm the other reason. A rancher named Butler Korne took me on as a green kid when I was one. I was happy there, the work was good and there were prospects. Nearly three years ago, the crew were in town on a Friday night. They were whooping it up, but I headed back early because I'd spent all the dollars I wanted to. When I rode in, I saw the boss – Korne – asleep on the stoop of his house, except he wasn't sleeping. He had a hole in him the size of a dinner plate. He was just sitting under the lamp, staring. It was where his killer had probably stood.' Billy stopped talking for a moment. Then he added a few more words for emphasis. 'The killer he must have known.'

'Is this where Quince comes into it . . . what it's all about?' Harmer asked.

'The safe was open and the following month's payroll was missing. When I told the Prescott sheriff my story, it was *me* ended up behind bars. But I've no chip on my shoulder for him. It did look cut and dried. Although he didn't do much to stop proceedings. I wasn't known as any sort of hellraiser, and I didn't have the dollars stashed away. I thought that would be enough to convince the jury.'

'But it wasn't?' Harmer wanted to know.

'No. Quince lied at the trial. He told them he saw me ride off after the shooting, even though he'd said he didn't know about it until the next day. How the hell was that? I asked. There must have been one hell of a gun shot. But no one was interested. They'd got me, and sentenced me. That was it.'

'What happened?'

'I escaped the day before I was due to hang. Been

on his trail ever since.'

'How'd you know it was him . . . Quince?'

'Only the killer would have seen me that night. There was no one else there. He's the one who said he'd seen me ride off, but he's the one who disappeared. And now we know how he got the money to set himself up in Pelicano.'

'He needs it. He's a man who has to pay heavy for whatever he wants,' Sarah said, quietly.

'Yeah, I understand,' Billy agreed thoughtfully. 'There's other people besides Butler Korne who'd want him brought back.'

Billy's voice suddenly dropped away, melding with the silence in the arroyo. No one spoke for a full minute, then Harmer, who'd been listening and thinking, cleared his throat.

'Fair enough. I reckon there's still one or two minor questions, but on the whole it's a good argument, Billy. Billy *Finch*. And if those Prescott lawmen don't believe it, hand the cur straight over to me,' he said resolutely. 'Now, I reckon that sky's staying darker for longer than it should. We should be gone.'

'We've got a tough ride. What'll be happening at Walnut Bench?' Billy asked.

'They've got Franklin Poole, God bless 'em. *Vamanos.*'

CHAPTER 10

The high midday sun burned on to the big slanting wedge of surface rock where the riders dismounted. Desert flats stretched out on all sides, white and glaring, unbearable to look at. Through a wavering sheen of heat, the tracks made by three bone-weary horses appeared to come from nowhere and to be headed nowhere.

Bigg Harmer's voice was a painful croak. 'How's our water going?'

The hands of the stem-winder blurred before Billy's eyes: 'Another hour before the next issue.' He spoke thickly, through split and swollen lips. 'Hell of a place to get us lost this time, Sheriff.'

Harmer snorted. 'It was either this way or mixing it with those *pistoleros*. Believe me, they're not our guardian angels. An' we're *not* lost. Just harder country, is all. They'll be hunting the likely trails. We had no choice.'

'I know,' Billy said ruefully. 'I'd probably feel a lot

better if those vultures weren't hanging around. Look. There must be a dozen, just watching an' waiting.'

Shading his red-rimmed eyes, Harmer peered up at the dark, featureless shapes wheeling slowly in the sky. 'There's four of 'em. They're turkey buzzards, and that's what they do. They want dead meat, not the living.'

'Yeah, that's what worries me,' Billy said.

Harmer squinted ahead. 'When we get off these goddamn flats we can rest up before making the Whitewater.' The sheriff stared biliously at the big man slumped on Billy's dun mare. 'Why the hell don't you make him walk?' he rasped. 'Take some lard off him.'

Quince raised his head, no longer sleek and well maintained. 'I know what's stuck in *your* craw, Harmer,' he responded.

'You don't, you son of a bitch. If you did you'd be seriously thinking of taking your own life.'

'That daughter o' yours,' Quince continued. 'She pestered me to take her away. Her arm didn't need twisting.'

'Shut it, Quince. So help me. . . .' Harmer threatened.

Quince looked at his soiled, store-bought clothes. He rubbed his hand on the dirt-smudged trousers, looked mindfully out across the salt flats.

'One night at my hacienda, your daughter drank too much,' he replied. 'She fell over a balcony and

110

broke her neck. That's the long an' the short of it, whether you like it or not.'

'You put out it was a low, dog-hole drinking house.'

'No I didn't. That was added by someone to give it some pepper.'

'Ah, shut it, you lying pig.' Harmer turned away from Quince. 'Hey, Billy. Even if you get this trash all the way to Prescott, he's not going to talk a rope off your neck on to his own. Have you thought about that? Why not leave him here? Take the girl – Sarah – and push to the river. That's what I'd do.'

'Don't listen to that ol' wit stirrer.' Quince stared at Billy, saw the cording of his neck muscles.

'While you're sitting there, he's the eyes in the back of my head, Quince. Don't forget that,' Billy said. 'And you'll talk all right when I get you to Prescott. You'll tell everyone what really happened.'

'Sun gettin' to your brain, is it?'

'No, not yet. Just think about me leaving you here, Quince. Leaving you with a bitter old sheriff who don't care much about his life any more, except vengeance . . . settling a score. Out here all alone, no friends, no guards, lookouts or gunslicks. Think about it.'

Harmer laughed. 'Hey, you're making it sound real fun, Billy.'

Quince went silent. His head and shoulders slumped, his eyes lifting to the waterless flats. Nothing much lived out there. He could see the bleached bones of some nondescript animal, and his tongue suddenly felt thicker and dry. Overhead the buzzards still circled. They were a tad lower, he imagined, and when he looked at the bones again, he thought they might have been human.

Billy snapped shut the case of his stem-winder. 'We'll have a couple of mouthfuls each,' he said, unplugging the canteen. 'No more.'

Tyler Quince watched Sarah Munnies take her drink. Then his scheming eyes followed on to Harmer, who licked his cracked lips.

'Here,' said the sheriff and held out the canteen. 'We mustn't forget the animals.'

Quince pushed it to his mouth, held it up and gulped, drank greedily and gulped again.

'Hell, you really are ridin' your luck, Quince,' Harmer rasped and made a swipe for the canteen.

'Listenin' to you an' Finch, maybe I can afford to,' Quince answered back.

Billy stepped in and took the canteen. 'That's OK. Your next drink won't fill the mouth of a rock lizard,' he said, 'And I wouldn't rely on that immunity from getting hurt. My tolerance has just started to wear thin.'

Quince sniffed uncaringly, turned to face Sarah. He grinned, his eyes tracing a line along her legs, holding a long moment somewhere above her knees.

Harmer was watching. 'I guess she'd be promised

airs and graces . . . a life on the plush, same as my Raphy Rose,' he suggested to Billy.

'She needn't worry about that any more,' Billy said. 'Like us, it's dying out here,' he added with a meaningful smile.

Harmer coughed. 'Yeah. I'm thinking, from now on, perhaps you shouldn't let Quince see so much o' your back.'

'How far d'you reckon we are from knowing we're going to live?' Billy asked, after taking his measure of water from the canteen.

Harmer looked up, pointed a knotty finger at the eastern horizon. 'That sky looks ominous. Underneath's what they call the purple haze . . . sagebrush. There'll be habitation of sorts, and water.'

Billy shook the canteen. 'Let's hope so. We've just about run dry here.'

'It's no more'n ten miles to the big river, after that. We'll make it,' Harmer said.

Tyler Quince ground his teeth, looked back at the barren reaches they'd crossed. A vein pulsed in his temple, and he closed his eyes as if willing his men to rise up from the sand. He paced slowly for a while, then hunched down near Sarah. Billy and the sheriff would be beyond earshot if he spoke quietly.

'I'm thinkin' I've seen those pretty long legs before,' he said.

Sarah pulled herself away. 'Keep your wretched thoughts to yourself,' she snapped.

'Yeah, I've seen you at work. Much further north than here, o' course. Billy Finch know you're one o' them frail sisters, does he?' Quince smirked. He enjoyed the distress he was causing and continued needling. 'Taken a shine to you, young Billy has, that's for sure. What was the establishment called? The Red Shoes? A cunning name for a cheap liquor an' whore house.'

Sarah forced herself to look at him. 'Cheap enough to attract *you*,' she hissed back.

Quince was grinning, contempt showing in his eyes. A blister beetle landed on his stubbled chin, crawled steadily up towards the corner of his mouth.

Takes one to know one, she thought. Both poisonous. . . .

With a fast movement, Quince caught the insect. He made a fist of his hand, listened to its buzzing attempts to escape, and held it towards her. 'Remind you of anything?' he asked, nastily.

'You know what you're *not* getting, mister, so what is it? What do you want?'

'A gun. Those two have got enough between 'em, including my Walker. It shouldn't be too difficult. Ha, you can certainly get close enough,' he said, easing away from the shady side of the big rock.

'I can stop him talking, if you want,' Billy called out.

'No. He won't ever be botherin' me.' Looking

up, Sarah saw Quince squeeze his hand to crush the beetle.

'We've run dry,' Harmer said. 'We can't stay here.'

CHAPTER 11

After leading the horses for the last few miles to the northern edge of the salt flats, the desert travellers warily considered the tumbledown buildings ahead of them.

'That really is a two-by-four outfit, and it looks deserted,' Billy said. Then he turned to the storm cloud that was pressing in from the west. 'I don't want to be standing here when *that* arrives.'

'Nor me. I've seen those beasts uproot cotton-woods.' For some time Harmer had been keeping an eye on the dark, grey-yellow colour the sky had turned. 'It'll be an hour still before it touches us.'

The tinny sound of a small clanging bell suddenly interrupted the ominous silence. Billy scanned the rickety smallholding. 'What the hell's that?' he uttered. 'I hope it's not the wind devil,' he said, looking at Harmer.

Breaking through the dry brush, a sancho goat stretched its neck and looked at them suspiciously.

Then it ran on and others emerged, followed by a Mexican who was shouting and brandishing a shepherd's crook.

'Pronto. *Esta manera,*' he urged his flock before seeing the four Americans. He stopped, dropped the crook and made the sign of the cross. '*Amigos.* I am a *cabrero* . . . a poor man.'

Harmer laughed. 'So are we, compadre. We're not going to hurt you. We just need shelter till the twister blows over. You understand?'

Noticing Sarah Munnies, the peon's trembling eased a little. He looked up at the darkening sky and blinked. '*Sí amigos, yo comprendo. Mi tortillas es su tortillas.* I will be one minute.'

Billy and Harmer exchanged a quizzical look between the peon and themselves.

Re-armed with the crook, the Mexican chased his small flock of goats into a sparely built pole shelter. The animals had started to bleat nervously and he was gulping, breathing heavy. He saw Billy hauling a bucket up from the well and waved his arm.

'*No tiempo,*' he protested. '*No tiempo.*'

'We came all the way across your goddamn flats on one canteen. There's time enough,' Harmer corrected.

'I have water in the house,' the peon replied, the first harbinger of the wind blowing against his thin poncho. '*Por favour.*'

Billy released the crank handle and the bucket fell back with a splash. Dust was now gusting, rising

117

in distant clouds. 'The bad bit's a good twenty minutes off,' Harmer said.

'The hell it is,' Billy guided Sarah at a run for what looked like the goatherd's dwelling.

Tyler Quince lingered. His hopeful eyes were intent upon something out across the flats. A moment later, a gunshot rolled in. It reached his ears above the low soughing of the wind, and he could make out a handful of riders cutting fast through the llano.

The irony of the gunshot wasn't unnoticed by Bigg Harmer, who gave a thin smile. 'Attaboy . . . good memory,' he muttered. The lawman's Colt swung to point the way to the Mexican's cabin. 'You're going with *us*, Quince. An' if you think we need you alive, you got it wrong – a fact I haven't mentioned to Billy. Though I'll only do that if I shoot you. And the longer I look at you, it's more *when* than *if*.'

'What the hell are you talking about?'

'I'm the sheriff of Walnut Bench. An elected authority of the law who can ride to Prescott and testify about you confessing to a murder. That means, Billy don't actually need you, and I'm real close to putting a bullet in you. They're not good prospects. So you can get inside, or I do my part *now*.'

Quince started to walk ahead of Harmer, and tried an upbeat, over-confident laugh. 'They're my guns, Sheriff. Be like cornerin' a coon.'

Billy emerged from the Mexican goatherd's doorway. He looked towards Harmer, then beyond him. 'Was that a gunshot?' he asked.

'Yeah, a message from his paid guns. They've doubled back. Smarter than I thought . . . don't give up so easy.' The hard-faced lawman quickly planted a boot behind Quince's knee. 'If only I could lift my leg higher. . . .' he rasped irately.

'. . . and he was facing you,' Billy added. 'I'll go bring in the horses.'

'No need,' Harmer told him. With their eyes rolling in alarm, the three mounts were walking to where they could see and hear the men talking.

'They've probably sensed what's going to happen,' Billy said. 'The safest place for them is where we are.' Ignoring the peon's protests, Billy led the horses inside. After Harmer and Quince entered, he slammed the door against its leather hinges and dropped a stout, wooden lath into its holding brackets.

Drawing his Winchester from its scabbard, Harmer stationed himself at the single front window, saw that Billy was casting a doubtful look at Quince.

'Don't worry about him,' he said. 'We've had a talk.'

Billy stood beside a narrow aperture that had no glass, just a sacking curtain. 'This'll be them,' he observed, and threw his sombrero to the ground. 'I've got my own hat. Reckon they know by now we're not of their breed.'

Five Mexican horsemen had left the flats. They walked cautiously forwards until they were just outside the range of any hidden guns. One of them spurred his mount a little ahead, looked up and shouted.

'Send out Señor Quince. The rest of you Americanos carry on up to the border.'

'He's going to Hell. *Infierno*,' Harmer railed back. 'So you all ride back to where you come from, unless you want to go with him.'

'Ah, we are sorry, gringos. But we have already been paid for this. It is a matter of pride, you understand. The *orgullo*.'

Within the deep shade of the cabin, Tyler Quince responded. With a short cough of laughter, he bared his teeth and yelled: 'Pancho? Forget your goddamn pride and shoot. Kill 'em before they do for me.'

The stock end of Harmer's Winchester drove any further words and several teeth back into Quince's mouth. Trying to split blood, the man held up a hand as the rifle swung back for another blow.

'Just one more sound . . . .' Harmer snarled. 'Get down and where we can see you.'

With a painful groan and a mouthful of mashed teeth and gums, Quince buckled to the hard-packed dirt floor.

The peon stared imploringly from Billy to Harmer to Sarah Munnies. 'Who are you all?' he asked. 'What are you doing here? It's only me and my goats. I want no trouble.'

'None of us wants it,' Harmer returned sharply. 'We're all at the wrong place at the wrong time. For that I'm sorry. *Lo siento.*'

As a timely reply, puffs of cordite smoked above the horsemen who had been steadily riding forwards.

'Now they're in range,' Billy shouted. A fusillade of bullets smashed open the poorly made door, the wooden planks breaking apart and splintering across the room.

As the *pistoleros* circled the cabin, Billy steadied his Colt on the window frame's sill and fired. His shot found a target and one of the Mexicans flipped from the saddle. 'One down, four to go,' he called across to Harmer.

Hurt, shocked noises came from the sheriff as exploding glass shards slashed his face, the bullet zipping close by his head. He tried a speculative reply shot, ducked again and more glass flew. 'Sons of bitches,' he cursed. He turned to the window again, triggered off a close pair of shots. But the riders didn't falter in their purpose and he whirled away as more lead seared the heavy air. With his back against the wall, he wiped blood from his face and reloaded.

Tyler Quince now sat in the darkest part of the room, head bowed, fists clenched in nervous anticipation.

Harmer watched the goatherd, who was pacifying the horses. The Mexican shook at each gunshot, huddling close in a corner where death or injury was most unlikely to happen. Sarah Munnies was crouching close to Billy, ready to pass him the Winchester when his Colt was finished.

Her face registered fear, but there was also an edge of doggedness. Harmer had seen it and he warmed to her. He rolled his shoulder along the wall, turned back into the window space and fired. But Quince had seen the rifle in Sarah Munnies' hands, and thought he had a chance. Behind the backs of Billy and Harmer, who were returning serious gunfire, he eased himself closer to Sarah.

'Hand me the rifle,' he said in a low-pitched voice. 'Put it on the floor, an' I won't tell Billy boy about what I know.'

Sarah knew immediately she was going to call his bluff. After all, he was the only one without a gun. 'Tell him!' she answered back. 'Right now I couldn't care a monkey's!'

Quince cursed. He lunged over to her, clamped his big hand over her mouth, stifling her cry. He twisted her round, down and closer to the ground, his other hand reaching for the Winchester. He wrenched it from her grasp, twisting her head up, gripping her ever tighter.

Sarah wanted to bite, yell for Harmer or Billy, but they were still heavily engaged and she had to handle it herself, think of some other way. Unable

122

to open her jaw, she lifted her hand and dug her fingernails into Quince's neck, dragging them roughly along his thick neck. Enraged, he pulled her to the ground, used his bulk to pin her down while he quietened her.

'Leave the *señorita* alone,' a voice croaked into the mayhem of sound.

Quince looked up and hissed at the trembling speaker: 'Beat it, *dago!*'

The peon, fearful and uncertain of what he could do next, darted a fast, nervous look around him. Outside the wind was rising, starting to blanket the racket of incessant gunfire. Quince was beyond reason, and in panic he turned the rifle on the slight Mexican. 'Goddamn peasant,' he rasped and pulled the trigger. At close range, the rifle bullet tore a big hole high in the peon's chest, smashing him lifeless into the fresh horse dirt.

Sarah screamed with revulsion. Quince swung the rifle towards Bigg Harmer, the long barrel glistening in the choking gloom as the sheriff turned. Quince guffawed crazily as he squeezed the trigger a second time.

But Billy had reacted. The full weight of his body crashed into Quince, sending the rifle bullet harmlessly into the low, frail structure of the roof.

Quince fell heavily against a clay oven. It went over, the cold ash spilling across the already soiled, bitter floor. Billy picked up the heavy pot lid and slammed it hard against the side of Quince's face.

'That's from all of us,' he ranted.

As Quince fell, Billy dropped the broken lid and kicked him in the ribs. 'You'll not be any more trouble,' he continued, with a brutal punch down to the back of his neck. 'Not again. Not to anyone.'

Billy leant down, and with both hands grabbed Quince by the shoulders of his jacket. He lifted the man and turned him on to his back. He took him by the shirt collar with his left hand, and hit him with the right. The man's nose crunched broken and flat with the first punch, and Billy hit him again, harder.

It took another frantic yell from Sara Munnies before Billy let go of Quince and took a step back. 'My friend Butler Korne, the sheriff's daughter, and now an innocent goatherd. Who else?' he raged. 'You want he should live to do it again?'

'No, Billy. I want *you* to live. If you kill him with your bare hands, you'll die too. A bit.'

'She's right,' Harmer supported. 'If there was any doubt about him not being guilty before, there isn't now.'

'Yeah.' Billy stretched the fingers of his right fist and winced. 'Killing's too easy for him . . . too painful for me.'

'Besides, we still got those lice of his to deal with.'

'Sounds like they've lost interest. That, or we've all got another enemy.' Billy waited until Harmer was back beside the window, then he picked up the Winchester and handed it to Sarah. 'If he tries anything again, blinks or makes a sound, hit him with this. Anywhere except his brain area should hurt. You can do that?'

'Yes. I can do it.'

Something in Sarah's voice made Billy look more closely at her. 'Did he hurt you? What is it?'

'Nothing. He didn't hurt me,' she replied. It didn't sound completely true, but there was nothing Billy could do about it.

'And keep away from the window openings,' he said.

The air inside the cabin was now rank, murky with the sweat and manure from the frightened horses, the adobe dust, blood and gunsmoke.

Billy was wondering why the pistoleros weren't all over the place, using the cover of the billowing dust. He aimed and fired at what looked like a figure sidling round the goats' corral, but the hammer of his Colt clicked on empty. He cursed, knowing there was nothing left in his gunbelt.

'Sarah,' he said, 'throw me the rifle.'

He took the Winchester, steadied himself against the opening and waited. But nothing moved. 'There's bullets in Quince's belt,' he yelled. 'You know he won't hurt you. Fill the Colt.'

The wind was rising now, coming in hard from the north-east. There was no other sound, everything had turned silent. Billy looked at Harmer, saw the sheriff's troubled face.

'What?' he mouthed. Harmer shouted something back, but Billy only heard the chilling sound of wind. Harmer held up his rifle, shook his head and Billy understood.

Sarah was standing close. Staring horror-struck through the window, she held Billy's Colt down at her side. For a short moment, on the edge of a spinning whirlpool of dust, they saw a man and a horse vanish from sight.

The frail adobe walls of the cabin started to shift, then parts of the sod roof broke apart, and lifted like a pie top. Billy cursed a few words of prayer, looked reassuringly at Sara – and then dust and darkness enveloped them.

CHAPTER 12

From a crouch position, Billy pushed up the brim of his range hat, squinted at where the roof had been. 'Gone,' he said incredulously. 'What the hell happened?'

He looked around the room. One of the side walls was half missing, suggesting the direction the wind had taken. A swathe of destruction flattened the earth outside, the pole corral was razed to the ground, and the goats were missing.

'We came through,' Bigg Harmer snorted, banging thick dust off his clothes. 'I didn't think these old bones would ever tread US soil again. You all right ma'am . . . Sarah?'

'I've managed everything that's been thrown my way so far,' Sarah replied. 'And that includes continually being taken advantage of.'

'I haven't taken advantage of anyone,' Billy coughed out, freeing a protecting arm from around her shoulders. Harmer and Sarah exchanged a light, perceptive smile, more a nervous relief at their shared survival.

Tyler Quince was propped up on one elbow. He was blinking slowly and tentatively holding fingers to his smashed mouth. Billy just stared at him for a moment, then, toeing aside bits of the shattered oven, stepped to the rear of the cabin.

The three horses stood loosely roped. But they held their heads close together, very still and fearfully wide-eyed. Beyond their feet, covered by a skin of fine, powdery dust, Billy saw the insensible face of the peon staring up and back at him.

'We've still got the horses – if they let us ride 'em,' Billy said grimly. He fixed Quince with a cold, hostile stare. 'We're going to make it, even if we have to drag you,' he threatened.

'My men are out there,' Quince slurred.

'What men? Right now, there's not a living soul within ten miles.' Harmer sneered and pushed at the remains of the door. He watched it crumble from its hinges, a mix of dry wood, sand and adobe dust puffing into the brightening afternoon. 'Even gophers'll still have their chuffs tight shut,' he said.

'Get to your feet, Quince,' Billy's voice interrupted Harmer. 'Get these mounts outside. You've got fifteen minutes to see they're ready for walking to Walnut Bench.'

A couple of minutes later, Billy and Harmer approached the well. 'Let's hope there's more'n pit vipers down there,' the lawman offered hopefully.

Billy hauled up the bucket, and Harmer grinned. 'Looks like we got the breaks.'

'The breaks?' Billy echoed in some surprise. 'Where've you been the last day or so . . . the last hour?'

'Hey, someone must be looking out for us. We're still alive aren't we?' Filling the canteens, the sheriff noticed Billy's attention was drawn to the cabin. 'There's something else?' he asked shrewdly.

'Maybe.'

'Maybe . . . certainly. Funny how priorities change, eh Billy?'

'How'd you mean?'

'Hell, the girl hasn't looked anywhere else since we first met up. What's troubling you . . . apart from the obvious?'

'I'm a goddamn criminal. A no-good fugitive of the law. Prospects aren't a glittering prize, either. So, any thoughts about Sarah Munnies. . . .'

Harmer grunted a sound of understanding. He flung the filled canteens over his shoulder, gave the serious-faced young man a quick, but more penetrating look. 'Think, long term,' he muttered, before walking off.

An hour after riding away from the goatherd's devastated cabin, they topped a sandy ridge and looked back briefly. The turkey buzzards had returned, circling ever lower above where the flattened buildings would be.

A shudder ran through Sarah Munnies. 'I

129

suppose there's always something for them to eat
... somewhere.' Trying not to think about the dead
peon, she spoke quietly and to no one in particular.

'Fifteen miles to go,' Harmer estimated. 'A hell
of a route, but we'll likely make it.'

The weary sheriff had assured them the river lay
ahead. But all they could see was a burnished sun,
rocky hills strewn with purple sage. Single file, they
followed on towards the Whitewater.

Dusk caught the tailing moon, but before full dark
they'd splashed across the river. The world was
warm and muggy, quietly humming with the sound
of shallow running water and night bugs.

Bigg Harmer dismounted with a sigh, sank to his
knees and patted the ground. 'We'll camp right
here,' he said wearily. 'I want to be fresh ... real
hair-triggered when I meet my deputy.'

Billy nodded, had already dragged Quince from
the saddle. Keeping an eye on him, he untied the
lariat from the back of Sarah Munnies' saddle.

'Throwing her a pack hitch?' Harmer asked light-
heartedly.

'It's for Quince,' Billy replied bluntly. 'From now
on there's no unnecessary risks. This rope'll give me
a rest.'

'Yeah, squeeze him up good an' tight. We don't
want him able to swat these goddamn skeeters
away.'

'No one's layin' a rope around me,' Quince

uttered. He took one step, turned, and lurched away two or three more.

Billy cursed and moved quickly. He lashed out a foot and Quince tripped. Before his shoulder hit the ground, Billy was bending over him.

'In case you'd forgot, you're not going anywhere, and you don't have a say in anything,' he said roughly. He tied Quince's arms behind him, running the rope down and around his knees and ankles.

'Yeah, trussed-up better'n a Thanksgivin' turkey,' Harmer growled. 'I'd have included his neck, though. Have you done ropework before, young feller? Beeves . . . horses, maybe?'

'Not horses,' Billy said abruptly. 'I'll get some brush for a fire.'

'I'll come with you,' Sarah said.

'If you want.' Billy walked off into the darkness with a thought to pick dry touchwood from the flotsam above the waterline.

'Billy?' Sarah called.

'Yeah? You got something?' he asked.

'Not really. Never mind.'

Billy was going to reply, but when he saw Sarah walking away, he too changed his mind. The Whitewater was flowing peacefully, bright clouds from the big dark sky mirrored in its surface. Along the shore, Billy snatched up brush, kicked at the sandy ground.

*

Billy's harsh expression softened as he looked across the glow of the campfire's embers. Sarah Munnies' flaxen hair was fanned against the seat of the saddle. One hand was pale, looked soft, peeking from the saddle blanket.

Tyler Quince wasn't full asleep. He was kept restless and uncomfortable by taut loops in the restraining rope.

'You should be more careful,' Bigg Harmer said to Billy. 'You can't treat a lass's feelings like that . . . hog-tied.'

Billy poked a stick into the fire, cast another look towards Sarah. 'I'm not treating her any way. Why should I be?'

'Just because. . . .' Harmer replied. 'Hell, you said yourself, you're something of a no-good,' he added with a smile. 'But that's not the same as saying *none* o' you's got any worth. It just needs some working on. Still, if I was ever stuck in a big ol' molasses barrel, there's no one else I'd sooner have along.'

Billy grinned. 'I guess you mean *me*. Well, likewise, Sheriff,' he said. Then he observed: 'You have thought about your deputy, haven't you? That he won't expect you turning up,' he asked, studying Harmer's craggy features.

'Wretched son-of-a-bitch,' Harmer snorted. 'He'll have the blind staggers just wondering where Ike Delgado is . . . waiting to get tapped for the bounty.'

Billy smiled coldly. 'I hope he gets to bed good an' early.'

'Yeah. Tomorrow's going to be a long day in the life o' Deputy Franklin Poole,' Harmer grunted.

CHAPTER 13

The rooster crowed and flapped its wings, strutted against the distant horizon. The rooftops of Walnut Bench's low-lying buildings were sharply outlined against the grey eastern skyline. The bird crowed again, and in the main street, yellow lamplight flickered through a dusty window.

Lowering the funnel of the oil lamp, Franklin Poole tossed a match on to the desk, and watched and waited until the small flame burned itself out. It was another dark blemish in the mahogany top. There were other nicks and gouges, most new, all tokens of Poole's huffy retaliation against a man and his office.

Poole dressed. He pitched water into his face from a basin, lifted a stained towel. He looked in a mirror, gingerly pushed a finger around dirty teeth. He was avoiding the badly set nose-bone, cursing at the memory of the fist of the man calling himself Bill Newton.

The deputy sheriff took a gunbelt from a peg on the short rack of hand guns, looked at the pendulum clock. It was already more than five hours into the day that Ike Delgado should be riding into town to collect his blood money on Bigg Harmer's death. He smirked greedily at the thought of the dodger he'd seen that said Delgado was worth five hundred dollars, dead or alive.

Minutes later, Poole put on his Stetson and doused the lamp. He opened the front door and stepped into the approach of first light, thought he would make an all's well, token round of the somnolent town.

The clock above the bar of the Cabaña ticked towards noon. The match in Franklin Poole's fingers trembled as he lit his wrinkled cheroot.

'And again,' he called to the barkeep. Impatience curled his lip and he drummed his fingers as his glass got its refill. 'Come on, I haven't got all day,' he muttered unpleasantly. 'Have I ever told you how to sell more o' this belly wash?' he asked.

'Can't say I recall,' the barkeep lied.

'Fill the goddamn glass,' Poole spat with no hint of good humour.

'Sorry,' the barkeep said, and pulled a few more drops of beer into the glass.

Poole downed the beer in one long, continuous pull. 'Hell, this would take down a goddamn buffalo,' he snarled. 'One o' the first things I'd do

135

as sheriff, is close this joint and run you and yours out o' town.'

'Bigg Harmer likes it here,' the barkeep offered.

'Well, he won't always *be* here. Then I'll find a reason, don't worry,' Poole replied and walked to the door. He kicked against the batwings, stepped outside – and stared along the street towards Ike Delgado's horse.

But after the longest moment, Poole let out a line of obscene, disbelieving curses: the man who was sitting in the saddle of Delgado's horse didn't have a slight frame, his features weren't gaunt, and he wasn't wearing a narrow-brimmed Derby. Hardly giving a glance at the three other riders, Pool turned on his heel and shouldered his way back through the batwings.

'Get me that big Winchester shotgun I know you keep behind the bar,' he commanded. 'Act dumb, an' I'll come round an' beat your head in with it.'

The barkeep was going to protest, but the words died in his mouth and he reached under the counter.

'An' keep your mouth shut,' Poole warned as he grabbed the shotgun.

The deputy walked quickly to the rear of the Cabaña and out, slamming the door shut behind him.

Heatwaves danced in the fusty air between the rear of the stores, and Poole continued to curse feverishly as he stumbled along an adjacent alleyway. The fear was making his heart thump. He could feel it pounding his ribcage, surging the blood around his temples, singing in his ears. *Harmer's alive*, his body was screaming. *Goddamn son-of-a-bitch Harmer's still alive.*

Trying to gain an idea, he stopped for a few seconds to stare at a rickety flight of stairs. 'So *I'll* shoot you. I'll shoot you here,' he muttered aloud, loping up the steps. He climbed over the top rail, stood on the ledge between the shakes of two sloping rooftops, and looked down on the main street.

Sweat soaked the upper part of his body. With his right hand he knuckled his eyes, watched the traffic below. Wagons, carts and buckboards rolled slowly along, while townsfolk, just as unhurried, lingered beneath the occasional shade from an awning. Looking for scraps brushed off the raised board-walk, a ribby dog skulked along one side of the street. Clap-boarded stores and offices were built hugger-mugger, no more than three feet between each one. If anyone had bothered to look up, they would have seen Poole stepping between them, moving further along the street – but most people weren't going to raise their eyes much when the sun was at its peak.

Bigg Harmer frowned at the cigarette burns that scarred the surface of his desk. He looked at the sagging canvas cot and two empty cells, and trembling with anger, he went back to the street and shouted at Billy.

'Looks like he got wind of my return. Knew what was good for him.'

Billy nodded. 'Maybe. And maybe he saw us coming. You can accommodate Quince for a spell?'

Harmer looked at Tyler Quince. With his dark stubbled jowls and haunted eyes, the rancher under duress no longer cut such an imposing figure.

'Sure,' the sheriff replied. 'I'll lock him up for as long as it takes.'

Untied, Quince walked straight into the first cell. Harmer booted the door closed, made play of turning the key. He watched Quince slump on to the cot, snorted drily between the bars. 'This is the time I now an' again feel a twinge of commiseration for the prisoner,' he said. 'But not today. I thought you should know that, you son-of-a-bitch.'

'A trapped rat's dangerous,' Billy cautioned. 'But all of a sudden, he don't look much of a threat.' Billy then glanced quickly at Sarah Munnies. 'Besides, tomorrow morning he'll be my worry. We'll go to the mail station. There'll be a coach up to Phoenix, and that's within fifty miles of Prescott.'

Harmer sank into his swivel chair, turned slowly, thinking. 'Quicker and easier if I make a telegraph call. The lawmen'll come collect if they know where you are. God's country it sure ain't. But for *them*, Walnut Bench is a few days out of the office.'

'That's a good idea, Sheriff,' Sarah said a little

uncertainly. 'I'll come with you if I may. I live near Wickenburg, so it can be me who takes the coach.'

Harmer looked from Sarah to Billy, couldn't stifle a low chuckle at the discomfiture. 'It's not exactly what I had in mind, but it's an idea,' he said. 'What do you think, Billy Boy? Good idea or what?'

'It's definitely more convenient,' Billy managed.

Harmer puffed his exasperation. 'OK then, Miss Sarah. Let's be ready at sun-up,' he suggested.

Sneery laughter drifted from the cells. 'You'll be stuck in the craw o' them Prescott boys, Finch. They'll want to string you up, an' I'm not goin' to say anythin' to change their minds.'

Billy cursed savagely under his breath. His fists clenched, knuckles whitened.

'Easy feller,' Harmer said. 'He'll sing like a canary when the time's right. Meantime, why don't you rid yourself o' that fancy dress? And the beard.'

Billy grinned. 'Yeah. It's beginning to feel like I'm carrying half a country in dirt around with me.'

'We've got a small stopover place with a bath-house behind it,' Harmer continued. 'I'll probably be visiting it myself shortly, ease some o' this gut pain. As Sarah will be needing a room for the night, why don't you both go over there and get yourselves sorted? I've got to tend to one or two things here.'

Deputy Poole nestled the shotgun stock against his clammy cheek. He squinted along the sights of the barrel as the figures emerged from the doorway opposite, drew a tighter bead on the taller figure of Billy Newton.

But it was Bigg Harmer he wanted first, and a shot now would lose him the edge of surprise he needed. He let the barrel drop, watched as Billy and Sarah Munnies walked towards Dormido House. He considered a smoke, but returned his attention to the doorway of the sheriff's office. Sooner or later Harmer would appear, if only to quarter the street. Settling to wait, he reached inside his shirt pocket for a crumpled cheroot.

Billy Newton had already discarded the sombrero. Now he removed the suede chaqueta, threw it across the painted screen that separated two bathing rooms. He eyed the foamy soap suds that brimmed the tub and gave a detached smile. He stepped into the water, sat down, closed his eyes for moment and relaxed. Less than a minute later he gulped, and flinched when a cotton skirt swung over the top of the screen, closely followed by a plain-looking chemise. He wanted to call out something, couldn't think what it might be, when what was unmistakably a pair of ladies' drawers followed.

'Billy,' Sarah Munnies called.

'Yes ma'am?'

'I'd almost forgotten what bathing was like.'

'Yes ma'am. Me too.'

'It's Sarah. Remember?'

'Not in here it's not, ma'am.'

140

'I've dropped the soap,' Sarah complained with an amused sigh.

Billy thought of a reply but didn't use it. He looked up at the Chinaman who appeared with a steaming kettle. 'It's hot enough,' he said with a shake of his head. 'I'm mostly flesh, not a pair o' miner's pants.'

'Billy?' Sarah called out again.

'Yes ma'am?'

'If Quince tells the truth, it'll put an end to your life as an outlaw. Have you given any thought to what you'd do then?'

'I have. Practically every hour of every day for two years. I know I'm closer to it, but there's still a chance he won't say anything.'

'You told the sheriff you were a rancher?'

'Not quite, I didn't,' Billy replied. 'Top hand was more like it. But right now I'm still riding the owl-hoot, and any hothead can pull a trigger for a reward.'

'There's a reward notice on you?'

'On Billy Finch, yeah. Sheriff's got a copy.'

'Why hasn't he done anything about it?'

'He likes me. Besides, he wanted me to go with him to bring back Tyler Quince. "Bring back" being an imprecise obligation.' There was silence for a few thoughtful seconds, then Billy continued: 'If I'm still asleep when you leave tomorrow, we'd best say goodbye now. Do you hear me, ma'am ... Sarah?'

'Yes, I heard you, Billy. And I've found the soap,' Sarah answered in a whisper.

Six hours of waiting had cramped Franklin Poole's legs. He'd lain in wait for Harmer, but in doing so had got himself trapped. It was cold now on the rooftops, his breath was making vapours, and he shivered. A small pile of cheroot butts littered the wooden parapet, the last smoked before any sort of darkness befell Walnut Bench. The deputy got to his feet hesitantly, stretched, then hunkered back down. He stared at the law offices, the square of yellow light beside the front door. Occasionally a shadow passed by one way, then the other. Poole wondered if Bigg Harmer was pacing the room nervously.

Changing his position, Poole leaned the shotgun against the sloping tiles. He realized that, when the door opened, Bigg Harmer would be standing against the light, and a perfect target.

CHAPTER 14

On the low cot, Tyler Quince shifted uncomfortably. From lying face down he grunted angrily and rolled on to his side, then on to his back. Eventually he swung his legs over the side and sat up.

'Hey, Harmer,' he rasped. 'Ever since Andersonville, prisoners have got entitlements, and bein' tortured ain't one of 'em. Why don't you keep still? Just for a few minutes, goddamnit.'

Harmer stopped pacing. 'Oh, you'll get what you're entitled to, Quince. Just got to be patient, that's all.'

Quince stood up from the cot, his fingers flexed, gripping at the cold iron bars. 'He's got to you, hasn't he? You couldn't care a tinker's damn if it was me or him killed that rancher. That's not what it's about, is it, Sheriff?'

'If you had more'n a couple of brain cells, Quince, you'd know it was Billy Finch who saved your life. If it wasn't for him ... if he hadn't

143

changed my mind, your *pistoleros* would be pullin' you along on a spade, or slappin' you down with it. And don't think it still can't happen.'

'That's an interestin' thought, Harmer. But what's tuggin' your chain, is your daughter. Her death was an accident, a misfortune. She fell to her death. I reckon it could even o' been suicide. That's unlawful killin' too, they say?'

'There weren't any witnesses to say anything.' Harmer took a step towards the cell. 'You made sure of that.' The colour drained from Harmer's face. He shuddered with emotion. 'Billy's got some real hard bark on him, but he's no outlaw. I've spent enough time with him to know that.'

'Maybe you're right,' Quince muttered, backing off into deeper shadow. 'Billy Finch has been wronged by me ... wronged badly. Tell you the truth Sheriff, it's been playing on my conscience. Perhaps I've got a chance to make things right with him. You know, if I'm going to meet my maker an' all. If you've got pencil an' paper, I can write something.'

'What the hell are you talking about?' Harmer rasped.

'I'm serious. Perhaps I can get me a ticket for the Redemption Pike. One sort o' confession's the same as any other, eh? It'll be enough for young Billy Finch to walk free.'

'You're crooked and devil-ridden, Quince. More than I thought possible. But I'll do it for Billy.' With

144

shaking hands, Harmer rummaged in the desk drawer. He pushed aside wanted dodgers for Pinky Grill, July Grant and Clayton Coyle. *Huh, Delgado was right about you,* he thought of Coyle: *I wonder where the hell you are now?*

He found a sheet of usable paper and a pencil stub, shouted threateningly to the man behind bars. 'If you back out on this, I'll feed you alive to John Chinaman's hogs. Broken up a bit, but still alive, so help me.'

'You'll get your piece of evidence, Sheriff. Don't worry.' Quince nodded earnestly as he got slowly to his feet, his slack muscles tightening.

Harmer's attention was momentarily diverted as the key grated in the lock. He took one step inside the cell and hesitated. 'What are you up to?' he said, instinctively dropping the pencil and paper, holding up both hands in defence.

Glancing off the edge of his right hand, the three-legged stool crashed against the side of his head.

Quince's burly weight went behind the blow, but it was diverted, glanced off hard bone and Harmer didn't go down. With tough old legs keeping him up, Harman saw the hazy, swimming countenance of Quince swing the stool again. He made a desperate grab, and his strong fingers grasped two of the stubby legs. He held on as long as it took him to reel backwards and reach for the iron-framed doorway. Quince kicked him in the stomach and pain

145

exploded deep inside him. With the paramount thought of stopping Quince from escaping the cell, he held on. He gasped in pain, tried to lift a leg, a foot for protection as Quince pounded him again with the stool.

Harmer wondered for the shortest moment on the whereabouts of Franklin Poole. *When did I ever need you?* he thought, as his muscles numbed and his mind started to fog.

Quince rushed at him, cursing. 'Damn you, old man,' he roared, his boot swinging up, low into Harman's ribs. With his stomach wound burning with pain, a choking gasp exploded from the lawman's lips. He hung on stubbornly while Quince now drove a tight-balled fist hard at his head.

Seemingly inured to the beating, Harmer's mind was still working. *If I can make it to the office*, he was thinking. *If I can make him follow me. If he makes it through the door, an' I get to the gun rack soon enough, he's mine.*

The grip of Bigg Harmer's hands broke free. He dropped away from the cell, falling back on to the boards of the office floor. Above him Quince grunted, stepped towards the sudden apparent freedom.

Tyler Quince was a younger man, bigger and heavier by many pounds. But Harmer was like a piece of jerked meat. And he knew more, and had done more, and it all counted. Dribbling, spitting blood, he forced himself to his knees. But as Quince reached the front door, he toppled sideways. With a remaining vestige of strength, he clamped his jaw and pushed himself up again. 'Quince, I promise there's a hell waiting out there for you,' he said between gritted teeth, as the escaping man wrenched the door open.

A single gunshot confirmed Bigg Harmer's chilling prediction. He stared in disbelief through the open doorway, saw a clenched fist, part of a dark sleeve stretching back into the wedge of yellow light. It didn't make instant sense, but at last he got an idea of where Franklin Poole was.

'The cowardly son-of-a-bitch is still out there. Got to be him,' he seethed. He stumbled from the office to the boardwalk, cursed when he saw a flick of Quince's hand. 'He's still alive,' he said, looking around him as though for support. He looked back down at Quince, took in the glazed, trapped look.

'How'd you do that?' Quince asked quietly.

'I didn't. An' it's not what we had in mind.' Harmer saw a dark, syrupy pool oozing its way down the heaving shirt front. 'Looks like you been hit in a bad place,' he said flatly.

'Yeah. Won't be goin' anywhere with you after all. Was it Finch?'

'No. It was my deputy. He thought it was me comin' through the door. But then it could be anyone you've ever come in contact with.' Harmer bent in closer to Quince. 'In a just sort o' way,

147

they've already been more successful than me or Billy.'

Another bullet smashed into the wall behind them. But this time a bright flash from the rooftop opposite indicated where it came from.

'If you're thinkin' of moving around, don't. You'll probably get another bullet, or someone else will. I'll send for the doc,' Harmer said.

Harmer had shuffled to one side when a third bullet hacked a big splinter of board from where he'd been standing. 'Ol' Frank must've realized it *weren't* me,' he muttered.

The window to the office blew out as he limped his way to the rifle rack inside the office. 'I'll take the building apart if I have to,' he vowed, reaching for the Spencer buffalo gun. He fed the single-shot breech with a cartridge, allowing the smallest of icy smiles to crease his pain-filled features.

The rifleman was still firing, but now more in hope than targeted calculation. A bullet thudded directly into the office, another smashed the face of the pendulum clock.

Going to all fours, Harmer made it to the front wall of his office. Outside, Tyler Quince was dying on the boardwalk, along with Billy Finch's future. The sheriff stood up. He lifted the Spencer to one side of the window and knocked glass shards from the bottom corner of the frame. He breathed out, aimed and fired, and took out a handful of wooden shingles from the roof of the mercantile store.

Walnut Bench had been suddenly and rudely awakened. The main street had cleared fast, on both sides, a few windows starting to flicker light, raised voices sharing shock and alarm. With his gunbelt in his hand, and chased by the yapping scavenger dog, Billy was running towards the sheriff's office.

'Stay over that side,' Harmer shouted at him. 'It's Poole. He's above McArdle's.'

Billy jammed his Colt inside his belt. 'Keep him there,' he replied, spotting the rickety flight of stairs that Poole had used earlier in the day.

Harmer's next shot coincided with Billy's leap up to the third or fourth step. Billy waited until Harmer fired again, then went straight to the top. As Poole had done before him, he climbed over the top rail and stood on the ledge between two buildings. But there he stopped. *Nearly got you*, he thought. *There's no other way down.*

Well away from the action, townsfolk were gathering below. Some pointed up at him, and Billy knew that if Poole saw them he'd probably guess what was going on. He drew his Colt, methodically set the action.

Tucked in behind the mercantile's upper parapet, Poole realized the gunfire had stopped. He peered over the bullet-chewed wood, but the dark emptiness that now filled Harmer's office window told him nothing. Harmer could be inside reloading, or watching and waiting from anywhere below. Poole pushed himself up a little higher, wondered if he'd actually hit Harmer. *No. This ain't the way it's meant to pan out,* he decided.

Across the street, Harmer kneeled. He steadied his rifle against the top edge of the desk, drew a bead line through the window up to where he'd seen Poole's shadowy figure. 'This'll keep your head down,' he whispered and squeezed the trigger. The satisfying, metallic clunk sounded but the gun didn't fire. The firing pin had snapped into a dud cartridge. Harmer drew back the hammer again and fired. But there was still no response. The breech was jammed.

Franklin Poole had seen the metallic glint, guessed at the misfire of Harmer's buffalo gun. 'Goddamn museum pieces,' he muttered with relief. He was hoping the saloon's Winchester shotgun wouldn't take on a similar fault – just as a harsh command cut the air behind him:

'Don't do it, Poole,' Billy rasped. 'Throw it to the street.'

The warning drew an instinctive response from the nerve-wracked deputy. Half turning, he swung the long barrel towards Billy.

But Billy had been ready. He wasn't waiting to see *if* Poole turned to fire, just the moment *when*. He got the moment right and fired a single shot.

Poole took the bullet high in his chest. 'It was nothin' to do with you,' he mouthed, dropping the gun because he didn't have the strength to throw it.

He collapsed sideways as one leg buckled, wasn't alive long enough to see the low ledge as he fell to the street below.

'It's Frank Poole. It was him doing the shooting!' someone shouted from the sidewalk.

'Whoever it was is still on the roof,' yelled another. 'Sheriff's coming out. Let's get over there.'

Bigg Harmer walked from the office, kneeled uncomfortably beside the prostrate figure. Quince's skin already carried a chalky, graveyard look.

'You don't need anythin' to write with. Not any more,' the sheriff said. 'Just tell me about Billy Finch. Say the words.'

'Go to hell.' Quince's voice was little more than a gurgled croak.

'There's good time for that, Quince. But not before you've told me what should be known ... what really happened.'

Harmer looked up, saw the townsfolk timidly crossing the main street. Billy was pushing through them, the fretful desperation clearly showing on his face.

'You used to be a gambling man, Quince. Let's see how much you can tell me about that night.'

'What the hell's gamblin' got to do with it?'

Harmer looked up at the questioning faces peering at him. Sarah Munnies was there, standing close to Billy.

'Going with the odds of gettin' it done before

your last breath. Now, tell me what really happened.'

'Ah, what the hell,' Quince started, closing his eyes for a moment. 'O' course it was me killed Butler Korne. I knew where he'd be . . . stackin' and restackin' his wads o' money. The crew was in town. I couldn't resist it. I was eatin' the man's dirt for five years. Finch made straw boss near soon as he got there.' Quince grimaced, slowly opened his eyes. 'I arrived with nothin' . . . sure as hell weren't leavin' the same way. I took what was mine, goddamnit. Finch rode in afterwards.'

The dying man's eyes flickered a final time. 'Where the hell's that doc you sent for?'

Harmer took his time in answering. 'I forgot. In the excitement an' all.'

The sheriff took a long look at Quince's dead body, then looked up at Billy and nodded. 'It's over. This time it's not just your word. There's witnesses to the fact, an' that includes me.'

'Thanks, Sheriff. One hell of a way to do it.' Billy then turned to Sarah Munnies, met the penetrating gaze she fixed him with. 'Now you know I'm saved, you can head for home. I can say goodbye, while I walk you back to the boarding house.

'Here is just fine, and you already have,' Sarah replied. 'Good night and goodbye, Mister Finch.'

Bigg Harmer leaned against the post of an overhang, looked at the people who were standing watching. 'It's your town. Some o' you get this vermin off the street,' he said. 'Get 'em both in the livery an' off the ground. I won't be here tomorrow, but Finch will handle things until I return. Sitting down an' doing nothin' for a few days sounds like a real good, timely idea.'

Billy offered a tight grin. 'I owe you that,' he replied, looking towards the Dormido's front steps. 'And I've just realized there's a personal matter I should have taken care of.'

'Yeah. Should have,' Harmer agreed.

Long before first light, Billy was sitting at the end of his bed. He was listening as the sheriff knocked on the door along the hallway. Ten minutes later, he heard the sounds which meant Sarah Munnies was leaving. 'Damn the old mulehead,' he muttered in the darkness. 'He knew I'd be sitting here twiddling thumbs, too chicken to say or do anything.'

He leaned towards the window and pulled the blind back an inch or two, was staring into the distance long after the dust from the departing mail coach had settled.

CHAPTER 15

The days which followed hung heavily on Billy
Finch. Walnut Bench was ordinarily a peaceful
town, and he spent most of the daylight hours
either patrolling the main street and its alleyways,
or seated alone in Harmer's office. One time he
even had a go at clock repairing, but without proper
tools it was a thankless task. During the hours of
darkness, his shadow wavered restlessly along the
boardwalks looking for wrongdoing, but there
wasn't any. Most townfolk were still only too aware
of the gunfight, weren't about to put any trouble
Billy Finch's way. By the time Bigg Harmer got back,
peace and quiet had got Billy more nervous than
facing bullets.

'How long you been running from the law...from
Prescott?' were the first words from Harmer on his
return.

'Glad to see you too,' Billy replied almost testily.

'Two years. Why?'

Harmer removed his hat, scratched his stubbly grey-haired head. 'Because for the last few weeks you've been running for no reason.' The sheriff perched on the desk, banged the calloused palm of his right hand down on the assembled documents and circulars. 'You've not been an outlaw, or any sort of fugitive, for more'n a month.'

'Who says?'

'There's law offices in Prescott papered with pardon notices. Here.' Harmer pulled a folded piece of paper from his coat, and handed it to Billy.

Billy read then swore. 'How come this didn't reach here? Why isn't it among all this other stuff?'

Harmer shrugged. 'I guess, lettin' us know who they want's more important that lettin' us know who they don't. Hell, Billy, you were a free man when you rode into town. Mexico wasn't necessary.'

Billy looked steadily at the sheriff. 'Maybe. For you it was. What happened?'

'It was after I gave one of the marshals the full story. Hah, he had to think twice about counter-signing my expenses.' Harmer smiled, sat in the chair Billy had vacated. 'It was a showgirl Quince stayed overnight with. After a few drinks, he told her he'd killed a rancher. She thought the name was Wheat, but it didn't take long for them to realize it was Butler Korne. Apparently she even had one or two greenbacks from Korne's safe . . . an' a clip he used to make 'em into bundles with.'

Harmer removed his gunbelt, draped it over an arm of the chair, and continued. 'Acceptin' it wasn't the girl herself – which the marshal did – from here on in, young feller, you don't have to start every time you see a badge. You can go back to being Billy Finch, not Billy Flinch.'

Billy raised an eyebrow, almost returned the smile. 'And that's all OK with you, is it, Sheriff?'

'Not totally. You'd never guess how Sarah Munnies had been earning her way.'

'No. I'd never really . . . .' Billy started.

Harmer held up his hand. 'If you had've done, perhaps the girl wouldn't be up in Prescott while you're still down here.' The sheriff swung round in the chair, reached up to the hat and coat rack and lifted the star from Billy's jacket. 'You won't be needing this tonight.'

'Why not?'

'Because you won't be here, goddamnit.'

Billy shook Harmer's leathery hand. 'Just one thing,' he said. 'There's a mare in the livery, and I'm kind of low on portable assets, so to speak. If you could see a way to . . .'

'Would a thousand dollars be enough for oats an' a good rub down?'

'Ten, was what I had in mind,' Billy said slowly. He was bemused, watching Harmer tip out a fat packet of bank notes.

'Some of this is yours,' Harmer said. 'An' please don't say, you can't take it. You'll never earn money

156

the way you earned this, believe me.'

'That's got to be true, Sheriff. For a moment I thought you'd said I'll never earn it going straight.'

Both men laughed lightly, embarrassed at their attempts to cover up sentiment.

'It's not like it's at the other end of the world,' Harmer came up with.

'Where *exactly* am I going?' Billy asked.

'The Red Shoes Saloon. It's at the north end of their Main Street.'

The sheriff stood out front of his office. He stayed until Billy ducked under the short rope that swayed above the entrance to Antigos Livery, and took the north trail towards Big China Wash and Prescott.

The barman of The Red Shoes Saloon looked up. 'I'd say beer, an' I'm usually right.'

Billy shook his head. 'Whiskey. The sort you don't keep under the counter, and fill the glass.'

The barman shrugged, tipped a nearby bottle and pushed the brimming glass across the counter.

For many seconds, Billy stood very still, seemingly considering the whiskey in front of him.

'Something wrong, feller?' the barman asked.

'I'm thinking about someone who works here, or used to.'

'Well they do say, thinkin' an' drinkin' don't mix. If he worked here, I'll know him.'

'Her,' Billy corrected. 'The name I know her by is

157

Sarah Munnies.'

'Hmm. You're wastin' your time thinkin' on that one,' the barman replied. 'But later on we got Big Lil an' Lil Big. They're somethin' special when they work together, if you get my meanin'.'

Billy picked up his glass and deliberately tossed the whiskey across the barman's shirtfront. As the man cursed his amazement, Billy tool a match from the bar box and held it up between his thumb and forefinger. 'Forget your sales pitch. Just tell me where Sarah Munnies is, or I'll light you,' he threatened.

'Hell, that's a new one, feller,' the barman conceded with a short backward step. 'Most o' the trade through here's liquor an' big wind. You're a bit different.'

Billy nodded quickly in agreement.

'She works down the street at the laundry. Yeah, I told her if she spends all her time there, she might wash away the uppity stuff.' The barman made a low sound in his throat when he saw the grind of Billy's jaw, the flat returned stare. 'Just a joke feller . . . didn't mean any harm by it. She weren't exactly a natural for this place.'

'Fill the glass again. You seem to have spilled the first one.' Billy swallowed the rough whiskey and smacked a coin down on the bar top.

'When I find her, I'll ask if you ever laid a hand on her,' he said.

*

At the laundering and clothing repair store, Billy removed his hat, waited a moment or two before the saleswoman plucked up courage to speak to him.

'Yes sir, what can we do for you today?'

'You have a Miss Sarah Munnies working here. I'm hoping I can speak to her for a few minutes. It's a significant matter and I've travelled a long way. I'll pay for any interrupted work, of course.'

'Oh, I'm sure there'll be no need for that. If it is only a few minutes, Mr. . . ?'

Billy just smiled inoffensively and she continued. 'Sarah's working in here at the moment,' she said, opening and closing a door quietly and efficiently as he stepped through.

He could sense the woman standing close outside, undoubtedly listening for some first-hand gossip. In front of him, at one end of a long bench, Billy saw a few piles of clean haberdashery. It would be ready for wrapping and collection. Another world, as far as he was concerned.

Sarah had her back to him, was standing in a smaller, hot-pressing room.

'Hello, I've come to see Miss Sarah Munnies,' he said. 'I've a problem she can run her iron over.'

'Billy?' came the surprised gasp.

'Sure is,' Billy grinned, taking a quick look around.

'What are you doing in Prescott? I would have thought it was the last place you'd want to be, now

159

you're a free man!'

'Yeah, well, that's the problem, Sarah. I really don't want to be. Not that sort of free, anyway. That's what I thought we could talk about.'